and the **PAULINE SOKOL** mysteries

Books by Lori Avocato

DEEP SEA DEAD
ONE DEAD UNDER THE CUCKOO'S NEST
THE STIFF AND THE DEAD
A DOSE OF MURDER

LORI AVOCATO

Deep Sea Dead

A PAULINE SOKOL MYSTERY

AVON BOOKS
An Imprint of HarperCollins*Publishers*

AVON BOOKS
An Imprint of HarperCollins*Publishers*
10 East 53rd Street
New York, New York 10022-5299

Copyright © 2006 by Lori Avocato
ISBN-13: 978-0-06-083700-6
ISBN-10: 0-06-083700-4
www.avonmystery.com

First Avon Books paperback printing: May 2006

Avon Trademark Reg. U.S. Pat. Off. and in Other Countries,
Marca Registrada, Hecho en U.S.A.
HarperCollins® is a registered trademark of HarperCollins Publishers Inc.

Printed in the U.S.A.

10 9 8 7 6 5 4 3 2 1

*To all the men, women, and children
whose lives have been touched by the sea*

Acknowledgments

To all my fabulous readers who have fallen in love with Pauline, Goldie, Miles, Jagger (Yum!), and the entire Sokol family. Without your dedication, there would be no Pauline Sokol Mystery Series. Thanks!

To all my family, friends, and fellow authors. You know who you are. Thanks for all the support and encouragement, and for keeping me writing. Oh, and listening to my complaining when I'm not in the mood.

To Jay Poynor, my agent, who has believed in me from the query letter on. Thanks, Jay.

Thanks, too, to Erin Brown, the most supportive and helpful editor ever! I appreciate all your input and the fact that you don't embarrass me when I write typos like locks instead of lox. Here's to many more books together!

Deep Sea Dead

One

"What? A boat? I mean a *ship*? I could fall overboard and drown! It could sink! Look at what happened to the Titanic!"

My skuzzy boss, Fabio Scarpello, glared at me with—well, one could never really know what Fabio thought, so I decided not to even guess.

It was more than likely X-rated anyway.

He puffed on a relit cigar. "The ship sails from New York to Miami to Bermuda and back. Who the hell ever heard of an iceberg in those waters?"

I wanted to argue that there might be pockets of cold water out in the Atlantic that could form into an iceberg, but I knew my imagination was just trying to come up with some wild excuse not to go. I wasn't going to mention my being prone to seasickness though. Fabio would turn that into something embarrassing.

After a few more puffs, he said, "Look, doll—"

"Don't call me *doll*. Ever." I sat straighter in my seat across from his mold-covered desk. Okay, maybe mold-covered was a bit strong, but I was guessing there had to be something growing beneath the used paper plates, coffee cups, piles of ashes and files. He had my folder in his hand.

"Okay, newbie—"

"*Pauline, Ms. Sokol* or *Investigator Sokol* will do fine," I started to sip on my decaf café latté that my coworker, friend and roommate Goldie had made me earlier, then decided it more than likely had been contaminated when I'd walked into Fabio's office.

He cursed under his breath. "*Investigator* Sokol is a stretch, but if you want to keep your freaking job, you better take this freaking case. High seas or not."

A nurse on a cruise ship.

I should have been excited about the assignment. I mean, come on. Salty sea air, wind in my hair, sun, bronzed males, coral sand of Bermuda and . . . waves. My stomach lurched.

And back into the old nursing career. That same career that I kept vowing I would never go back to. Damn.

He shoved the file toward me. "Want it or not?"

Not would have been my first choice. Pauline Sokol was not one for change. Pauline Sokol was not one for water transportation. And Pauline Sokol was not one to be stuck out in some nautical God-knows-where, investigating medical-insurance fraud . . . alone.

Admittedly, I've never been out of New England for a vacation or any other reason, and that probably had something to do with my reluctance to try new things. Hope Valley, a very "ethnic" community, had been my home for thirty-five years—and I kinda liked my feet on Mother Earth.

But there were those nasty things called bills that had invaded my life. And they required being paid. And that required money. *Sigh.* I looked up to see Fabio tapping his cigar into the dirty ashtray.

Amid the flying ashes, he asked, "Well?"

I snatched the folder. "When do I leave?"

"Friday."

"Friday? It's already Wednesday."

"One of the staff nurses onboard got, er . . . sick. It's perfect. Just perfect. Bon voyage, doll."

I decided to ignore Fabio calling me *doll* again since my mind got stuck on the word *Friday*. April 13. Perfect. My new assignment would start on an unlucky day. I hurried out of his office and paused in the hallway for a breath of fresh air.

"Suga!"

I spun around to see my tied-for-best friend in the world, Goldie, rushing down the hall. My other roommate and other tied-for-best friend in the world and Goldie's "honey" was Miles Scarpello. Fabio's nephew. Adopted. His saving grace.

There is a God.

Goldie dressed in Gucci, Prada and Armani. Sometimes from the ladies' department, sometimes from the men's. But I still loved him, and he always looked like a movie star. Today he ushered in spring with a pink, black, white and orange spiral-patterned sweater over black slacks and a pink camisole top. He wore a Sandra-Dee-blonde ponytail wig that looked more real than my natural blonde hair. Looked very sixties. And very beachy. How fitting.

Maybe I could borrow the outfit for my cruise.

"So, Suga"—he yanked me into his office, which looked like a cross between New Orleans (Goldie's hometown) and the jungle. Gotta love his unusual taste—"what's your new assignment?"

I held the folder out toward him as if it were a snake. "Here, *you* look. I don't have the stomach for it so early in the morning."

Goldie patted my head in a very Goldie-like sort of way. "Let's take a look-see." He ripped a pink-printed nail through the end of the envelope, and amid the tearing sound mumbled, "Shit."

"Shit? What does *shit* mean?" I slumped down on the zebra couch, feeling a bit faint. I think the color drained from my cheeks upon hearing Goldie's tone alone.

He looked at me for a few seconds. I had the sudden thought that he was making up some kind of lie. That hurt, but if Goldie lied to me, it would have been for my own good.

"I . . . well, what I meant was . . . Shit, you get to go on a cruise to some warm, sunny island, and I'll be stuck in stupid Hope Valley, Connecticut, with temperatures in the fifties all month." He took a gigantic swig of his coffee. Goldie never swigged.

I could only stare. Was Goldie really concerned with the temperature? Or had he seen something in the folder that I should be worried about? After several minutes of silence and then him offering me another latté over and over, I finally asked, "Gold, are you lying to me?"

"Yes!" flew out of his mouth on a breeze. He flopped onto his leopard chair and looked at me with a pitiable glare. "I'm sorry, Suga. But, Bermuda. *Bermuda!* Ber . . . mu . . . da!"

"I guess I'll give you credit for your honesty about lying even though I don't know what the hell you're talking about. As a matter of fact, I *will* take a regular latté, since I think I may need a dose of caffeine."

Before he stood he said, "Your standard at Dunkin Donuts is hazelnut decaf. You don't drink caffeine, Suga."

"I do now. Seems as if I'm going to need it on this case. What is so wrong about cruising to

Bermu . . . the triangle. You are worried I may get sucked into some paranormal triangle of ocean?"

Goldie screeched.

"I'm sorry, Gold." I jumped up and grabbed him in a hug. "I didn't mean to . . . Wait a minute. Why am I consoling you? I should be the one being comforted. I'm the one going on this fool assignment."

He eased free and looked at me. "I'm so sorry. I never should have said anything. I mean, folks sail to Bermuda every day. Planes fly overhead. And, well, bon voyage, Suga!"

"Bon voyage!" my mother shouted as she served me a piece of the ocean blue cake she'd designed for my going-away party. Inside was chocolate with a mousse filling.

All I could think when I heard that third *bon voyage* was, three strikes and you're *out*.

"Thanks, Mother," I mumbled as she set the dish in front of me. I loved cake. I loved sweets. I drank a very moderate amount of alcohol to avoid calorie overdose so I could have the sweets. Nothing could top chocolate. But right now I had this inner feeling telling me I should eat sweets like there was no tomorrow and drink plenty of liquor—because I was going on a cruise to *Bermuda*.

Not a worldly traveler, I did have a suggestion-prone kind of mind.

I remember once in grammar school when the nun told me I looked as if I had a rash on my arm. The idea ate away at me until a rash appeared. Of course, ever since she mentioned it, I had scratched at the skin over and over, even though it didn't itch.

My sister Mary, a nun herself—well, ex-nun now—leaned forward, pulling my attention back to the party. "You're getting to be such a professional with an exciting job, Pauline. Imagine. A cruise." She leaned back and shut her eyes. She talked a good talk, but I figured Mary was saying a Hail Mary for my safety. She never did quite lose that "religious" persona.

Several nieces and nephews stabbed at the cake's white waves fashioned out of cream cheese and frosting. Mother had outdone herself. Everyone ate and laughed and chatted.

I turned to see Uncle Walt, my favorite uncle who had lived with us forever, smiling. He leaned near and tucked a white envelope into my hand. "Meet some nice young man and have a ball." His bald head grew ruddy.

"I'm going to be working, Uncle Walt." I fingered the envelope. Had to be money. God bless Uncle Walt.

"Work. Ha!" He forked a piece of cake, ate it and said, "How sick can passengers get? A little sea-sickness? Meet someone. Dance. Eat. Old Widow Kolinsky tells me that cruises are the best. She said she danced so much heading to St. Martin, she wore out her shoes." He chuckled. "Wore out her shoooooes!"

I smiled, leaned over and kissed his cheek. "I'll be sure to bring a spare pair. Thanks for the gift." I winked at him just in time to catch Jagger in my view.

My face burned hotter than the candles on the cake my mother insisted on lighting even though I'd argued it wasn't my birthday. I hoped Jagger didn't think I was winking at him! I felt my tea rising in my throat at the thought.

He sat down opposite me and graciously smiled when my mother set a plate in front of him with half of the cake and a tidal wave of frosting on it.

"Here you go, Mr. Jagger," she said.

Actually she gushed like a teenybopper, but no way was I going to admit to myself that my mother was flirting with "Mister" Jagger! Yuck! Even though he had only the one name—that we knew about—she insisted on using the title. I couldn't help but cut her some slack because, well, Jagger had a way with women and obviously Stella Sokol was not immune. Guess I should have been glad my mother was a "normal" female and not think of his affect on her as icky.

"So, Sherlock, any questions before you set sail?" He took a sip of his beer. Gotta admire a guy who drinks beer with his cake—and damn, but I admired lots of things about Jagger.

I looked at him and realized that I was finally working on a case by myself. Jagger usually ended up involved. But not this time.

My heart skipped a few needed beats.

I was really going *on my own*.

Back in my condo, I flopped on my white-covered bed and looked into the dark little eyes of my joint-custody dog. Weighed in at seven pounds now after a doggie diet. "When's the last time a cruise ship sank, Spanky?"

He looked at me, curled into a ball, and shut his eyes.

"Right. The *Titanic*. Ages ago. I know there have been fires onboard and epidemics of gastrointestinal problems, but in this day of modern—" I hugged my pillow.

Spanky snored.

I had to smile while I petted his squirrel-sized head. "Modern technology. No problem. Where's my grocery list?" I leaned over, grabbed my paper and pencil and added *bracelet thingie for motion sickness*. God, I hoped the ship's movement wouldn't affect me, since admittedly, I couldn't sit in the backseat of a car without needing Dramamine. Damn.

Spanky snored on, so I continued packing, making sure to grab my stethoscope, bandage scissors and several pens. Back to nursing. I knew it made sense that my skills would be best suited to the medical-fraud cases, but hell, Jagger wasn't a nurse and he did fabulously. At least I didn't think he was a nurse. No one really knew who he worked for.

I'd learned not to care.

Besides, male-nurse Jagger? Naw.

After several hours, I stood back and looked at my luggage. Full to the brim. I used the extra strap, which wrapped around the bag in case the zipper popped, that my mother had insisted on buying after seeing it advertised on television. I assured her my luggage wasn't going to get thrown around like on an airplane, but being Mother, she had convinced me I didn't want the world to see my panties if, God forbid, the zipper gave way. Not that I expected that tragedy, but I'd learned from infancy that when Stella Sokol said something was going to happen, look out— because it always did.

As kids we used to cringe and fuss when she'd say, "Don't go out in the rain because you'll catch your death of a cold."

Even at our young age, we knew you had to come in contact with the cold virus in order to catch a cold, but inevitably, we'd go out, and the next day (always a Saturday), we'd get sick and have to spend our day off in bed.

So, I yanked at the strap to make sure my "essentials" weren't going to be exposed, and shoved the biggest suitcase with my foot until it was at the doorway.

Tomorrow Goldie and Miles would drive me to the dock in New York City to start my next case.

That alone was reason to lose sleep tonight.

My night was not as sleepless and fitful as I had expected. It was *worse*. But the next morning, once my roomies had the car packed—and they wouldn't let me lift a finger to help—we were well on our way.

The traffic on Interstate 95 was at its usual stand-still near Bridgeport, so I snuggled up to Goldie's shoulder while Miles drove. I shut my eyes.

"Suga. Suga?"

"Hmmm?"

Something nudged at my arm. I peeked out at Goldie and realized the car had stopped. I yawned, stretched—and screamed.

Goldie grabbed my arms and hugged me. "It just looks so big because we're so close up."

I looked out the window to see the "ship" I was going to be living on for the next few weeks or so—and strained my neck without being able to see the end of it. There had to be a million decks. "Don't heavy objects sink like rocks in the water?" I mumbled.

They laughed, and Miles gave me a quick physics lesson and assured me that the *Golden*

Dolphin, the mother ship of the Sailing Dolphin line out of the United States, was quite safe. Having done some Internet research about the private American line, he proceeded to tell us much more than we wanted to know.

I think Goldie even dozed off.

We shook him back to consciousness, and after Miles found a parking space, we all got out and stared at the ship.

The gigantic mass of white sat proudly at the dock, dwarfing the surrounding buildings. At least that's how I saw it from that angle. Hundreds of passengers were waiting in lines for what I guessed was some kind of processing before embarkation. We asked one of the staff what was going on and found out they were checking passports and getting credit card info and whatever else was needed.

I looked at my friends. "Well, this is it." After tearful goodbyes (mine) to Miles and Goldie, I turned to walk away then looked back. "I'm going to miss you guys." I sniffled.

Both had dry eyes.

Now that hurt.

And it really wasn't like them. Nope. Inside, they both had to be blubbering fools. "Well, I'll keep in touch, although I have no idea how—"

Goldie waved a hand. "I can't stand it any longer!"

"About time. I thought you two weren't going to even shed one tear to see me go."

They gave me a collective grin.

"What the hell is wrong with you guys? You're acting . . . weird. Weirder than usual." I chuckled.

Goldie grabbed my arm and spun me around. Despite my shouts to stop, Miles joined in the hug.

"What the hell? You're going to make me seasick before I even get on the ship." I yanked free.

Miles laughed. "You have your anti-nausea bracelet on. And"—he leaned near—"where'd you get that pink locket?"

"You like it?" I fingered it and smiled.

"It's you. Not too pretentious. Not too much like real jewelry."

"Jagger gave it to me. Inside is pepper spray. For self-defense."

They looked at each other and then back at me. "You won't need it!" they shouted together.

Once again they wrapped themselves around me, turning the three of us into a human pretzel.

"You guys are driving me crazy. What is going on? How do you know I won't need my locket?"

"Because we are coming along!" shouted Goldie.

Always, when Jagger said something to me that was a shock (and that was quite often), my mouth would drop open, and I'd stare into space. This time I had the same reaction, but then I let out a shout, "You are? You're coming with me?"

I looked at both of them and chastised myself for not being more astute. Miles had on white slacks, navy Polo shirt and sunglasses on top of his head.

Darling Goldie had the Sandra Dee outfit on, complete with blonde ponytail and a hat that matched the wild sweater. On his feet were flip-flops in the same colors.

Those outfits should have been my clue that they weren't just driving me to New York City. Damn.

"Yes! Yes! We are coming along!" Goldie shouted.

He proceeded to dance me around while Miles explained how they'd decided to take a much-needed vacation. In my heart I knew they were coming on the ship to keep an eye on my safety—and, hopefully, would not have to rescue me from getting sucked under by the Bermuda Triangle. I shuddered for a second, and then felt a sense of calm.

Gotta love those two.

"Gold, you really are making me seasick, and we haven't even boarded yet." He stopped the dancing and smiled. "I'm so thrilled." I stood on tiptoes and kissed each one on the cheek. "You guys are the best."

Miles put a protective arm around my shoulder. "You deserve the best, Pauline."

After a few more shouts and cheers, I left my friends to go get processed in as a staff member, with the promise that I'd find them later.

After I was checked in within an inch of my life by security, I headed up a slight incline of a gangplank. Once inside, I had to stop and take a breath. I wish I could experience this with Goldie and Miles.

The inside of the ship, like a lobby of sorts, was gold, purple, glass and chrome everything, and was decorated like a Las Vegas hotel. Glass elevators swam gracefully up the walls. Chatter filled the air, but in the background, soft music from a string quartet gave the *Golden Dolphin* the aura of what the *Titanic* must have been like.

The top of the ceiling was lighted glass in a very pale violet color surrounded by . . . more gold. Dolphins were painted swimming on the ceiling above, and it was as if the passengers were below the surface of the water.

Fountains in the center floor spouted colorful water shooting several feet into the air. Around the fountain were steps that led gracefully to a lower level. How fabulous.

For a second I couldn't believe I was actually still in New York City. No horns beeping. No sirens screaming. No "scents" of the city.

It smelled like a fresh ocean breeze.

After asking several of the crew for directions, I found my way to my quarters, which were located across from the infirmary on the third deck. Very convenient. The crewmembers had to live several decks below the passengers, and even had their own recreation spots, I'd been told.

I opened the door to see twin beds along two walls, covered in white spreads, in a room no bigger than a closet. The walls, too, were as white as the two stuffed chairs. I guessed the cruise-ship industry had cornered the market on white. Instead of windows, there were tiny portholes in the wall.

Oops. My claustrophobia came to mind.

I ignored it, telling myself this was a job. A job that I needed and *could* do.

On a desk near the portholes sat a note addressed to me. It was from the nurse I had to share the room with. She introduced herself as Jacquelyn Arneau and said she was French. No kidding. Real French, as in, came from France for this job. Seems as if the crew was a mixture of nationalities. Jacquelyn also said which bed she'd already claimed and that she hoped I didn't snore or spread anything of mine onto her side.

Suddenly I realized why the French were not number one on the list of favorite tourist nationalities.

Should be an interesting job.

Two

After unpacking what little I had brought on the ship—with the hopes I wouldn't be here long and maybe even have the case solved before the ship docked in Miami—I decided to walk the long hallways and do a bit of snooping while also trying to find what luxurious accommodations my friends had.

I knew my day of orientation wasn't going to start right away. My paperwork said someone would contact me after two o'clock, since the ship set sail at five.

My heart fluttered at the thought.

Ignoring an impending fear, I walked along the beige-and-gold carpeted hallway and retraced my steps until I was back to square one. I went to the reception desk, introduced myself, showed my ID and found out where Goldie and Miles were.

Before I knew it, I was on Deck Eleven, tapping

on the door to Penthouse Suite 1109. "Hey, guys, it's me."

The door swung open and Goldie, sans wig—which always gave him an eerie yet endearing look—pulled me inside. "Suga! Isn't this so much fun?"

I looked around their room. The main décor of burnt orange, deep reds, beiges and mint greens with stripes carried over to the gigantic king-sized bed and matching drapes. The suite was bigger than our condo at home. "Yeah, it looks like fun for you two. Me, I'm stuck in a sardine can of a room with a Frenchwoman who hopes I don't snore."

Goldie hugged me. "You *do* snore, Suga."

I rolled my eyes and pulled away, walking around their room in an envious trance. "My room is so small," I muttered.

Miles came out of what I peeked in to see was the bathroom, *without a* "folding" sink, and said, "Pauline, if you start to feel cramped in your room, just come up here with us."

I started to say I'd run and get my toothbrush and nightie right now, but instead said, "Thanks. I won't be in my room too much, since I'll be working."

Goldie gasped. "I hope you get some time to play with us."

"You and me both, Gold." I noticed they had fresh flowers and a fruit basket on a table near their balcony—and all I had was the note about my snoring.

Goldie touched my arm. "Before you get maudlin, let's go watch the people on the dock waving goodbye and pretend we know them. It'll be fun before you have to go to work."

I nodded and while they both changed, I walked around the room pretending it was mine and even went out onto the balcony and ate an apple from their basket—again pretending it was mine.

I had to get back to reality soon, so the three of us made our way down to the main deck, which was several floors above my cabin. On the way, Miles teased me that they had a balcony suite with butler service. I said that was because two guys could afford the Ritz with combined *male* salaries, and I again moaned and groaned at my tiny dwelling. We laughed and chatted all the way to the main deck.

As always, they made me feel much better.

I looked around the ship for as far as I could see. Even in the dead of winter in Connecticut, I've never seen so much white. White sparkled at me like a snowy day as we walked along the deck. Hunter green and white-stripped lounge chairs were lined up alongside the walls and were already filled with imbibing passengers.

The buildings of New York City made a picturesque background of grays and browns compared to the brilliance of the ship. Gold *everything* was the accent color of choice, with nautical navy-colored dolphins decorating the ship's outer walls.

We headed to the banister and watched as more passengers boarded. The excitement in the air was palpable, and I started to feel as if I were in some black-and-white (and gold) movie, waiting for Cary Grant to come strolling up the gangplank—if that's what they still called it. In fact, the ship sat fairly level with the dock so passengers didn't have to do any pseudo mountain climbing to get onboard.

Goldie placed me between the two of them as we waved to strangers below. I was kind of surprised that so many people had come to see the ship off, since·cruises were a daily occurrence around here, but I soon found out from one of the crewmembers that this cruise time was on the city tour map. The people below were mostly sightseers and had come to watch the ship set sail.

"It's still fun!" I shouted to Goldie and Miles.

Miles nodded. "At least we can pretend that we know the people madly waving to us."

We all laughed and shouted out various names as if we really did know them. I scanned the crowd and decided which ones were my friends and which were family. "That guy over there looks like my Uncle Walt," I said. "Hey, Uncle Walt! Bye!"

Miles nodded.

Goldie agreed.

I leaned closer. "Wow. He really does. And that lady—"

"Yoo-hoo! Pauline!"

I turned to my friends. "I think the sun is getting to me. I could swear I just heard my mother yoo-hooing!"

Goldie touched my forehead. "It's cloudy today, Suga. I think you need some medical attention yourself." We all laughed.

"Pączki! Pączki!"

Goldie leaned over the railing. "I thought I heard your father calling his nickname for you. You know, that word for the big, fat, round, prune-filled Polish donut."

"Pronounced like 'paunchki,' " I mumbled, afraid to admit that I'd heard it too.

Miles leaned closer to Goldie and pointed. "Yikes."

"What?" I bent to see where they were looking. "Oh . . . my . . . God."

Walking up into the ship was Mother, Father, Uncle Walt and some strange lady with blue hair. I collapsed into Goldie's chest.

"You think they are just coming to see us off?" I said in a pleading tone.

They both looked at me and said, "Do you?"

"Damn."

"I'd use something stronger than that," Goldie said in a very consoling tone.

"Pauline! Yoo-hoo! We are coming along. Uncle Walt got us a wonderful deal on eBay!"

eBay? Who knew Stella Sokol would ever utter the word eBay?

I forced a smile and watched my family walk onto the ship—and felt my insides knot up tighter than the sailor's knots in the ship's lines, holding us there in port.

"So, we decided we could all use a vacation," my mother said where we all stood in the ornate gold-and-purple lobby.

I realized what she said was a blatant lie. My parents were here to watch over me, just like my two friends were. I should be glad, but I had a job to do and didn't need any interference.

And oh, could Stella Sokol interfere.

I politely explained to my mother that this was a singles cruise, and maybe they'd rather wait for another one—as if the ships came in to dock like taxicabs.

She gave me one of those "Really, Pauline" looks and stopped me from arguing before I could open my mouth. Daddy was mesmerized by the ornate lobby and stood staring and silent.

Guess it wouldn't hurt to have them take a vacation.

Other than going to war in Korea, my father had never been out of New England either. And the farthest away from Connecticut that Mother had been was Maine.

A cruise with my family and two closest friends.

What could it hurt?

Who was I kidding? What could it hurt to have your parents on the same cruise as you, a never-married thirtysomething? And this a *singles* cruise, to boot. What if I really *did* meet Mr. Right, and my parents were along on what would then feel like a claustrophobic tiny vessel, which only held around 490 passengers and a little over 300 crewmembers?

Despite my logically knowing the ship was the size of Hope Valley, I felt like the walls were closing in on me because the entire Sokol clan was here. Okay, no siblings, but now I wouldn't be surprised if my brothers, sisters and their families climbed onboard too.

What the hell was I thinking, telling them where I'd be?

I leaned toward my mother, who was "yoo-hooing" to every gorgeous male (and there were scads of them) who climbed onboard. "Mom. Mother! Stop doing that. And, is anyone else coming onboard to 'surprise' me?"

Mother turned and grinned. At least I think she was my mother, but damn, outside of Hope Valley

Stella Sokol seemed a different person. "That's why you are still single, Pauline."

"Because I don't yell to strangers?"

She clucked her tongue. "Because you don't . . . Well, you don't let yourself go. Ever. Live a little."

I could only stare. The question "Who are you and what did you do with my mother?" sat on the tip of my tongue. But I couldn't even get that out. Let myself go and live a little? Suddenly the Bermuda Triangle was sounding like less and less of a threat, since now I was living in the Twilight Zone.

My relatives were all greeted, and everyone was ushered to their cabins by the staff. I wondered if I could avoid the Sokols for the remainder of their trip, but then reminded myself that I was talking about my *mother*. If any investigative skills came naturally to me, they had to be in the genes passed on by her. She could find a hidden cookie in a kid's sock drawer during a blackout while she had the cold of the century.

After we parted, I thanked the guy who helped me find my way back to my cabin. I unlocked the door and walked in to see several suitcases sitting in the middle of the room.

On the twin bed near the porthole lay a woman.

"Oops. Sorry." I checked the number on the door to make sure before closing it and assumed she was my roommate. "Hope I didn't wake you."

"Nope. I'm Jackie," she managed to say.

I walked closer and looked down. Her brown hair fanned across the pillow like a mermaid's. Deep, dark eyes that could be haunting if it weren't for the watery look that made her appear more ill than sexy. Her lips were colored in deep red, but smudged on the bottom, giving her a kind of glamorous hooker appearance.

"Pauline Sokol. I'm only filling in until they find a permanent nurse."

Jackie's eyes grew large, and then she merely groaned and shifted. "None of the medical staff is permanent. This month we get to sail with Dr. Peter VanHamon, a freaking OB/GYN from Minneapolis. Probably had some ER training in his past, but who knows how long ago. Dear Peter and I have sailed many times together. Cross your fingers that there are no cardiac problems this trip." She chuckled, then coughed and shut her eyes.

"Oh." Oh? That was all I could manage? Not wanting to stare at her, and reminding myself that she might be the one showing me the ropes, I looked out the porthole and thought of the doctor who could deliver babies for the swinging singles but probably not splint a broken wrist. Whoa! The skyline of New York City was moving!

I jumped and let out a shout.

Jackie grabbed her head. "Cripes, Sokol. I hope you're not going to act like some *femme* who's never left home."

I should have been insulted, but Jackie spoke in a French accent, so whatever she said seemed so impressive, I almost didn't care what it was. As I watched the Statue of Liberty get smaller and smaller, I said, "Sorry. Are you not feeling well?"

"Hungover, Sokolé. Nothing out of the ordinary."

I looked back and wondered why a beautiful young woman would drink so much that she'd look, and obviously feel, like crap the next day. "Did you party too much last night?" Everyone was allowed at least one faux pas.

"I didn't party at all."

Her tone sounded so, well, sad. I could feel my forehead crease, as she lay there with her breathing rather shallow. She moaned.

"I just assumed—"

"Do not assume anything around here, Pauline Sokolé. Nothing." With that she shut her eyes, while mine bugged out at the scary thought. It wasn't only what she said, but *how* she'd said it.

Suddenly my singles cruise of fun and bronzed men had become a cruise to hell.

I said a quick prayer to my favorite saint, Saint Theresa, that it would be a round-trip.

I managed to finish unpacking as quietly as I could while Jackie slept. I wondered what my family was doing, but knew I couldn't go traipsing about to find them. *What size was my parents' cabin?*

I wondered, then hoped it was nice and large, since they deserved to get away and have fun.

Only not on my cruise!

After there was nothing else to rearrange or unpack, I looked at Jackie. Maybe I should wake her to find out what to do to get to work.

Before I could, a knock sounded on our door.

I looked through the peephole to see a woman standing there. Dressed in white slacks and shirt, she looked as if she were in the Navy.

I opened the door. "Hi."

"Pauline?"

I nodded. "Come on in." Then I said, "My roommate is sleeping," as if the woman couldn't see Jackie passed out.

"I'm Betty Halfpenny. No relation to Moneypenny from 007." She chuckled while I admired her English accent. "Born and bred in London, educated U.S., nursing degree from University of Pennsylvania. Real name Elizabeth—no great surprise, with the queen and all—but to annoy my mum, I started calling myself Betty in my teen years and it stuck. Family has royal connections, but don't ask me about them."

In one hand she held a hanger of white clothing. She reached out to shake mine with the other. "Oh, these are yours. Put them on for a little orientation. They should fit. The paperwork said you were a bloody size four. I hope the trousers are not too baggy." She laughed. "No great surprise that Jackie is napping."

Betty was several inches shorter than myself, a few pounds heavier and had curly red hair, which went splendidly (I thought in a mock English accent) with the millions of freckles on her face, arms and neck.

I took the clothing and wondered what she meant by "don't ask about the royalty" part. Maybe she just didn't know that much about it. "Yes. Four. Thanks."

She looked at Jackie. "Did you at least get to meet her before she went to the land of Winken, Blinken and Nod?"

"I did."

"She's a great nurse, but sometimes has bad form. You know, has issues."

Issues? Hmm. Could be right up my alley.

In my past cases, I'd found that disgruntled employees often sang like canaries where fraud was concerned. I'd have to buy Jackie a drink tonight— if she sobered up by then—and hear what tune *she* sang.

All I knew from Fabio was that someone (and he never shared with me who it was) had reported possible fraud involving overcharging patients for medical care while out at sea and then skimming the difference off when the insurance companies coughed up the huge amounts.

Fraud cost the insurers thousands of dollars.

They kept raising their rates up and up so they wouldn't have to shoulder the losses, and as a middleman, it cost Fabio too. Nothing started his day off on the wrong foot like losing money.

All I had to do was find out the who, how and how come of this case. Ha! Nothing was ever easy in this business, but I figured there had to be a few folks involved, to pull off this kind of scam.

"I'll give you five to change in the loo, and I'll come back for you," Betty said.

"Thanks. Shall I wake Jackie?"

Betty shook her head. "Not that I think you could, but it's her day off. Always better to leave her be."

Thank goodness she's not on duty, I thought as I headed to the "loo" to change.

If the room we were housed in was tiny, and it was, the "loo" made my closet at home look like a sprawling mansion. The shower didn't even have a curtain on it, since the entire room was tile and the floor had a drain in the center. A sink protruded from the wall, but looked as if it folded back up to allow for more room and to shower. Although done in white tile, it sure didn't look like it belonged on the *Golden Dolphin*. I really was glad that my friends' and, hopefully, my family's rooms were 100 percent better.

I slipped into the freshly pressed slacks and button-down, short-sleeve shirt Betty had given me. Epaulets sat rigid on my shoulders, giving me the "Love Boat" of the late seventies look.

Actually I felt very professional, and told myself I really wasn't a nurse any longer. This was a disguise I was forced to wear to do my current assignment. And I knew just where I'd start.

I'd start with my orientation by Betty and work my way up to drinks with disgruntled Jacquelyn Arneau.

I had a gut feeling that would be when my *real* work would begin.

Three

I stood on my tiptoes to try to see myself in the tiny sink's mirror, since there wasn't any room for a full-length mirror around here. Damn, but a uniform did wonders. I looked spiffy in the white top and 'trousers,' as Betty had called them.

I had pulled my hair up to look more professional and thought I even looked a bit sexy. Neat. Couldn't hurt on a singles cruise.

When I came out of the bathroom, Jackie was sitting on the edge of her bed, and Betty was settled in the chair near my desk, looking at some paperwork. She looked up. "You look peachy, mate."

I smiled.

Jackie stared for a few seconds. "Yeah, *peachy*."

There was that accent again that made me unsure if Jackie was being flattering or sarcastic.

Betty stood and ignored Jackie, so I assumed there was no love lost between the two. Hmm.

There was also something else I noted about the two. I couldn't say for sure, but they occasionally looked at each other . . . oddly. It reminded me of the looks my sister Mary and I gave each other when we were keeping a secret from our other sister, Janet.

Secrets? Right up my alley.

Jackie collapsed onto her bed. "She has a right to know, Halfpenny."

Betty cleared her throat and gave Jackie a dirty look. That one I couldn't mistake for anything else.

Jackie curled her lips at Betty. "Tell her, or I will."

"Shut up!" Betty turned to take my arm.

"Excuse me," I said, to remind them that I was in the room. "Tell me what?"

Betty's grip tightened and then released.

Jackie sat up. "You're replacing Remy Girard. He and I went to nursing school together. Rem . . . Remy was a good friend." She curled her toes. Very gently she touched one nail with a finger and said something in French. I was guessing it was a curse, since the nail polish had chipped off the corner of her nail. Then she lifted her pillow to take out a picture framed in a brass holder.

I could see Jackie smiling at the man. Remy? He had on a crew uniform and, I noticed, one of those woven bracelets made out of some kind of rope.

Jackie had a similar one on her ankle.

Good friend indeed.

Betty took my arm again. "Let's go."

This time Jackie stood up. Make that, jumped up like a Jack-in-a-box. "She has a right to know!"

Oh, boy. "I'm getting confused. I have a right to know what?" My heart started a little arrhythmia brought on by fear. These two were driving me nuts. "Someone better clear this up soon, or—"

"Remy didn't get sick!" Betty shouted. I had only just met her, but the tone of her voice seemed very uncharacteristic. Especially for a polite Englishwoman.

Jackie let out those same French phrases and this time I was certain they were X-rated. "You are nuts, Betty." She turned toward me. "But she is correct. Remy didn't get *sick*. He . . . *disappeared*."

Betty gasped, followed by my gasp.

"You mean he fell overboard?" I croaked out.

The two looked at each other. "Maybe," Betty said.

"Unlikely," Jackie said right after.

I flopped down onto the nearest chair. "Well, what do you mean, 'disappeared'?" I had all kinds of visions of how I was going to kill Fabio and wasn't even open to the suggestion that he didn't know. Sick indeed.

Betty sat on my bed. "We really don't have any details, Pauline. Remy wasn't very happy the last few months."

Jackie grunted.

Betty turned to Jackie. "Well, he wasn't. No thanks to you." Then to me: "He might have jumped ship in Bermuda. We really don't know. Captain Duarte simply told the staff that Remy was no longer working here and would be replaced."

With me. Yikes!

Jackie looked at Betty and gave her a "so there, I got my way" kinda grin, then said, "I'm tired."

Betty ignored Jackie and looked at me. "I shall show you around the casualty now."

My eyes widened. "There's already been a casualty!" I hoped my friends and family were all right.

Jackie chuckled. "Bloody British with their own words. She means the ER, or actually the infirmary, as I call it."

Whoa, boy. "Ah. Great, Betty. Lead the way."

On the way out I noticed that Betty gave Jackie a look that said, "Freaking French." I only hoped I'd get along better with the two of them or I might not be able to concentrate on my jobs—nursing and investigating.

I also added finding out more about Remy Girard to my list.

Across the hallway was a set of double glass doors with MEDICAL CENTER written in black-and-gold lettering. Upon entering, I thought, *This dolphin décor has been a bit overdone.* The place looked more like a lounge than an infirmary.

At a violet-and-lime reception desk sat a young man dressed like us. Betty introduced him as one of the nurses. Enrico "Rico" Bono was Italian (but had lived in the United States since age nine) and was damn good-looking. Think Al Pacino minus a few years. Rico jumped up, hurried around the desk and took me into his arms. Yikes!

"Welcome aboard, Pauline."

He spoke like a regular American, kinda New York meets New Orleans, but the deep tone of his voice had me thinking I'd heard a sexy accent or maybe it was just because his breath tickled my neck as he spoke.

I looked at Betty. "Is it hot in here?"

She grinned. "Rico is on duty, so I'll show you around."

With that he let go but not after whispering in my ear, "I'll see you later, *amore*."

I didn't need an Italian/American dictionary for that term.

Betty's tour included the main nursing station and the one ICU room with all the equipment up to date. Tubes, wires and extra lights hung from the walls around the hospital bed. On the nearby crash cart stood a monitor and defibrillator. IV bags stood at the ready, hanging on nearby metal poles.

"Looks like the ER back home," I said.

"Precisely," Betty added then showed me all the supplies in a small closet near the porthole.

Green, peach and beige-stripped drapes hung from the sides of the porthole, making it appear more like a real window. The walls were painted a mint green, which gave them an air of comfort.

I sure hoped this room wouldn't be needed on my cruise.

"Those glass doors lead to a hallway where a lift will take you to the upper deck if a patient needs to be taken out by a helicopter. The pool has to be drained so no one gets electrocuted. Quite a bloomin' procedure."

"Hope it's not needed on this trip," I said.

"That's it for physical setup. Feel free to poke around yourself."

Just what I wanted to hear.

She continued, "Let me show you the procedure manual. Everything is spelled out quite nicely. Then I'll show you the schedule."

She pronounced it "shed yool." I had to smile. Seemed as if Betty could insult me too, and I wouldn't care. But she was so sweet, I doubted I'd have to worry. It was so much fun meeting people from other countries.

"On this line we work twelve-hour shifts. That way we are off more. More free time to sightsee or rest."

Or investigate, I thought. "Sounds perfect."

"You know we also treat all the crew. Three hundred of them. This is their only means of receiving routine medical care along with emergency care as needed."

I nodded, but hadn't been aware of that. Of course, what little Fabio could tell me about this job was . . . frankly, nothing much, other than I was to find out who was committing fraud and to save him money.

"You have a few days to review the procedures. We run things a bit differently on this line, but we do follow all the Healthcare Guidelines for Cruise Ship Medical Facilities. You'll start Monday at seven A.M. for your shift with Jackie."

Opportune moment here. "With Jackie? Hmm. She been here long?"

Betty hesitated. A telltale sign in the investigative field—however, I had no clue as to what it meant. I'd find out.

"Jackie's been on and off cruise ships— different lines—for years. I don't remember the last land job that she had. She probably doesn't either."

Interesting. "So she basically has no home port?" I thought that sounded very nautical, as if I knew what I was talking about.

"Jackie is . . . well, she's . . . yes, she really doesn't have a place to call home. She travels a lot."

"Kinda sad. I imagine she misses her family and friends. Not married?"

Betty gave me a "what the bloody hell are you

so interested in Jackie" kind of look, but ever-so-properly said, "Married about three times that I know of. Right now she's single, except for her boyfriend, Claude."

The way she said *boyfriend* made my eyebrows rise. "Is he on the crew?"

"Claude. Claude Bernard, her latest, is the crew's purser."

"Crew's purser?"

"Sorry. I forgot you are not up on the ship lingo. Crew's purser provides administrative support. Claude does the crew paperwork and assists in all crew matters. He also makes sure we keep our quarters in reasonable order."

I chuckled. "Guess I don't have to worry about that too much if Jackie is—"

"—Doesn't matter who sleeps with whom, Pauline, we still have to follow the rules."

Yikes! Put in my place, I fumbled for words. "Sorry," was all I could come up with.

"Anything else?" she asked.

I know she meant about the room, but said, "Did Jackie and Remy have a thing going?"

Betty hesitated. "He loved her."

That was it? In my book, that was enough. Hmm. He loved her, but Betty didn't say how Jackie had felt about him. Jackie certainly hadn't looked too upset talking about her "friend," and now she was already dating someone else. Interesting.

"Well, back to the tour," Betty said. "I relieve Rico in a few hours."

"Oh, sorry. Didn't mean to take up so much of your time off."

She waved a hand in the air as if I really hadn't and proceeded to show me the medications, which were mostly used in the management of common medical emergencies. Lots of cardiac meds, vascular, respiratory and plenty more. The ship looked very well equipped, and Betty seemed her usual pleasant self as long as Jackie's name wasn't mentioned.

"This area is where we keep all the laboratory (which sounded so British when Betty said it) equipment and in that room is the X-ray machine."

Chills raced up my spine. I'd had a bad experience in an X-ray room with a past case—actually, a dead body had the bad experience.

"Of course, the most popular drugs we hand out are antiemetics like meclizine, our drug of choice, and Dramamine. Seasickness and all." She chuckled. "We stick on a few plasters." She chuckled again.

Betty was quite jovial.

" 'Bandages,' as you Americans say," she clarified.

I had a sudden craving for tea and crumpets.

"I'm guessing the cruise line makes a bundle on those drugs." I studied Betty's reaction.

"Oh, no. Those are gratis."

Damn. "Makes sense. Guess if too many patients get seasick, the popularity of future cruises diminishes." Now *I* chuckled.

"Correct."

"So what about the other meds and treatments? How do we know how much to charge? How does that work?"

"Not to worry, Pauline. There is a staff receptionist that handles that type of thing. Medical staff don't stick their noses into billing."

Betty looked like she was in a hurry. Damn. I couldn't keep her there, since she probably had things to do before her shift. I smiled. "Okay, well. Guess I have enough reading to do, and if I come up with questions, I can ask Jackie."

"No! I mean, find me or Rico, and we'll be glad to answer them."

Rico came up from behind. More like snuck up from behind. Gave me the chills, but not the scary kind—more like the sexy kind. Felt good when he put his arm around my shoulder too. I told myself that sometimes I was pathetic, but that was the way of life for a thirtysomething single female nowadays.

"*Amore*, I am at your service."

I eased free and smiled. Okay, I eased free and smiled after a long pause. "Thanks. Well, guess I'll head off and do some reading. I also have some friends on the ship (admittedly a Freudian slip that I didn't say relatives too) and would love to meet up with them for a bit."

"Go ahead," Betty said while Rico nodded.

"Learn your way around. Get your sea legs," he added.

"Thanks. See you both around."

I hurried out the door and leaned against the wall, thinking, *Damn, but that Rico arm/shoulder thing did feel good.*

"Look at you in that outfit, Pauline," my mother said as I stood in the doorway of their cabin. "You look so nice, I don't see why you don't go back into nursing."

I didn't want to argue that looking good in a uniform was not a good reason to go back to a career that I had burned out of, so I eased past her and said, "Your cabin is wonderful!"

Daddy was napping on the couch near the sliding doors. I was glad they too had a balcony like Miles and Goldie's and mentioned that fact. Daddy snored in agreement and Mother came closer.

"White makes your skin look too pale though. Go sit outside for a while."

"It's cloudy, Mother. Besides, I only came to see your place." .

She leaned near. If she mentioned my skin or eyes or clothing again, I might be tempted to fling her overboard. "Isn't it like yours? Our cabin?"

I laughed. "Similar, but mine is for the crew, so it's a bit smaller. But very nice," I lied, after the thought struck me that Stella Sokol might find out my room number and come "help" make it better. "Very nice."

I walked toward the balcony, but decided not to step out. Looking at the land floating by, I told myself if I went out there, I'd miss having a balcony along with the opportunity to get fresh ocean air. Then, I might get the urge to come up here . . . and I wouldn't wish that on my enemy.

I was trying to wean myself from relying on my mother's pine-scented Renuzit, which gave me a nostalgic, comforting feeling. I'd been known to rush to her house for a whiff of family comfort after some traumatic incident—usually from this job.

Out on the ocean, I felt I could handle it all by myself.

And I was not going to even *think* about Jagger either.

Mother looked at her watch. "It is almost time for dinner."

Without looking, I knew it had to be nearly six, since my mother had a precise time for each meal. I wondered if she'd lighten up and relax on this cruise.

"Yeah, I'm getting kind of hungry." As soon as the words came out, I wanted to lasso them back in, knowing I'd left the barn door open and readied for the stampede.

"Perfect. You'll meet us in the lobby for dinner at six. Don't change, Pauline. You look so nice."

"I . . . I am part of the staff now, Mother. I have to eat with them."

"But it's a singles cruise."

I could only stare.

She looked at me as if I were a moron. "A singles cruise, dear. You could meet a nice young man."

Duh. "I'm here to work." I refused to tell her that I had been looking forward to meeting some bronzed hunk—and learning more about Rico.

She looked at my outfit. "Are you working now?"

"No. I'm off until Mon . . . oh . . . my . . . God." She had a way, a subtle way, of making us kids tell the truth when we least expected to. Damn.

"Mon? What does Mon mean? Monday? Don't talk in that kind of lingo and do not use the Lord's name like that either."

Did Stella Sokol really just say "lingo?" I think the ocean air was too thin for her mind. I hoped she was getting enough oxygen.

"So. Six it is. And wash up first. Do not eat at the buffets!"

"Mom, I—"

"Don't argue with your mother. I read that those buffets that everyone talks so highly about are what cause . . . you know the kinds of problems I'm talking about."

"Overeating?"

"Don't be rude, Pauline. I'm talking about all

the sickness that is so common on these ships. You never know who washed their hands before a meal and if they have touched the food. Oh, my." She shook her head.

I had to smile. "Mom, please try to enjoy yourself."

"Enjoy, *schmoy*. I suppose you think I'd enjoy myself after stuffing my stomach then getting sick the rest of the trip and living in the bathroom. Really, Pauline, you have been out of nursing way too long."

It had only been a few months, but I decided not to mention that fact. "So, where's Uncle Walt staying?"

"He's in the other room, Pauline."

My eyes widened. "You have *two* rooms?" It came out as if I was some nutcase, but in truth, I was just awed that they had two rooms and I had . . . the one with Jackie.

Speaking of Jackie, I had to head off and see what I could find out. I walked toward the door. "Tell him hi when he wakes. Daddy too."

My father mumbled.

Mother brushed some imaginary dust from the bedside table. At least I couldn't see any. Then again, I didn't have her "cleaning" genes. "Almost time for dinner, Pauline. Do not eat at the buffets around here," she repeated. "You never know who touched what. And if they washed their hands first."

"Yes, Mother. You mentioned that before." Suddenly I lost my appetite.

"Doesn't hurt repeating. Not all passengers wash their hands before meals. I read that before we came on this ship."

"Love you both," I said and hurried to the door.

My mother stepped in front of me. "You really do look nice."

I nodded in agreement (the only sensible thing to do) and ran out (the other sensible thing to do). Once in the hallway, I wondered, *What the hell did she mean by that?* Was mother just being nice or did she have some hidden meaning behind her words?

Pauline, I said to myself, *we're talking about Stella Sokol here.*

I went with hidden meaning.

On the way up to Miles and Goldie's suite, I told myself my mother was going to spend her entire trip trying to find me a husband—and I'd be sequestered on this damn floating singles prison until she did.

I shook my head as the elevator door opened—and I ran smack into a prospect. "Oh! Sorry."

The bronzed god caught me before I knocked him against the wall. With a face as red as a cooked lobster, I looked up at him. With shoulders like that, he couldn't be knocked into anything.

Well-built arms held me for a few more seconds until I eased free. He had on black shorts, a sleeveless black-and-white tee shirt and matching sneakers. Yikes he looked good.

"No problem." He leaned near and read my name badge. "Ms. Sokol. *Nurse* Sokol, I'm guessing."

"How did you know?" The elevator door started to close. The god stuck his hand out and it slid back into the wall. I don't think he even touched it.

"The uniform. I'm Hunter Knight. Cruise director." He held out his hand and the elevator door started to close again.

Since he ignored it, I went to grab for it. "You'll miss your floor."

He took my hand and said, "It'll be there."

The door shut.

My heart might have stopped for a few seconds. I wasn't sure, but I had all the symptoms, including that white light thing. Well, maybe that was the reflection of Hunter's teeth. They were damn perfect, as was the rest of his body, right up to the blond hair and blue eyes. Maybe contacts. But still looked good. Hey, we could all use some artificial help sometime.

The elevator started to move. I had to ignore it. Once I was stuck in an elevator with Jagger and I ended up passing out. Well, *stuck* was not exactly the correct term. He'd stopped it. I looked at Hunter and told myself Jagger was miles away and that I should just concentrate on the present.

"So, what do you think about the *Golden Dolphin* so far?"

"I . . . please press Eleven. Thanks." I eased back and realized the wall behind me was glass. The entire passenger population could see my butt pressed up against it even though covered in my whites. *Pull yourself together, Pauline.* "Oh, this is my first cruise, but the boat . . . ship . . . is wonderful. I mean you can't even feel it moving. It's so . . . lovely and the purple and green and gold and the passengers look so happy . . ."

I pushed away from the glass and looked to see Hunter grinning. Once again I had babbled uncontrollably in the presence of a gorgeous guy. I blamed the recent incident on my mother making me flustered.

I had to get "lucky" soon.

Obviously it had been way too long.

The door opened. "Here's Eleven." He held the door and said, "I've got all kinds of good things planned for this cruise. I hope you will join me in some of them."

My mouth went dry. Words wouldn't come until I ordered myself to say, "Sure. I'm sure it will be fun on my time off."

He smiled.

Yikes.

Before I stepped out, he said, "How about joining me tonight? I have a dance set up for welcoming the passengers. Lots of single ladies, so I've hired some male hosts—"

I felt my eyes widen. "Hired?"

He chuckled. "Not like I'm some pimp, Pauline. It's very common on cruises. Males are needed for escorts to the shows or to dance or just to have dinner with single ladies. I arrange that."

All I could say was, "I hope they don't have to pay for their trip."

He laughed and moved to the side. "It's taken care of. Part of the deal. Shall I pick you up around nine?"

"P.M.?" I had envisioned myself asleep by then.

He nodded. "I'll find your cabin."

With that I stepped off the elevator, not even realizing that I'd successfully ridden it without so much as a heart palpitation from my phobia.

The door closed behind me. I stood and looked around.

Suddenly I'd forgotten where I was or why I was there.

Four

"Suga? Is that you?"

I swung around to see Goldie, dressed in his Sandra Dee outfit and wig, coming down the hallway. Looked lovely and perky all at once. Now I remembered that I'd come here to see my friends. If I ran into any more bronze gods like Hunter and Rico, I might not be able to do either of my jobs.

"Oh, hey, Gold."

He grabbed me and swung me around. "Don't you just look precious in that outfit, Suga!"

I laughed. "Thanks. How are you guys doing?"

"Come inside. We are doing fab. Miles is down at the gym doing his Miles thing. I've been out looking at the scenery and planning our trip. This ship has a great cruise director . . ."

I know Goldie was still talking, but my mind flashed back to the elevator—and Hunter Knight.

"White knight in shining armor" came to mind, or maybe, since it was a swinging singles cruise, white knight *out* of his shining armor.

"Suga?"

I felt a tug on my arm.

"You all right?"

"I . . . met him. The cruise director."

Goldie whistled. "Ah. Now I see why the trance. Good. Keeps your mind off that dangerous yet infectious Jagger. You know he's not good for you—"

I didn't want to hear Goldie's usual "Jagger is like a drug" routine. He'll hook you and then hurt you. "He's not good for anyone. I know. Yes, I met Hunter Knight. As a matter of fact, I'm meeting him tonight—"

"Yippee!" Goldie shouted.

A young couple walking down the hallway hand in hand turned and smiled.

"You go, girl," Goldie added, a bit more controlled. "I have a very good feeling about this cruise, Suga. Just what the doctor ordered."

"I thought you were worried we'd get sucked into the Bermuda Triangle." I chuckled.

Goldie waved a hand. His nails matched the pink in his shirt perfectly. "Sometimes we have to take our chances in life. It's time for you, Suga. Time."

Time? Hopefully it wasn't my time for . . . you know. "Hey, Gold. Listen to this." I told him about Betty and Jackie being at odds, not wanting to tell me something, and then dropping the bomb about the missing nurse.

Goldie shrieked, oh-so-very-Goldie-like. "Suga, you have to find out more. A missing nurse? It sounds as if there is more deception going on around here than just your fraud case!"

"That much I already knew. Actually, there has to be much more going on around here. Neither women seemed . . . scared. They were more evasive, as if hiding something."

Goldie hugged me. "You be careful—and wear your pink necklace."

I laughed. "I thought you and Miles were here to protect me, but I guess you're too busy having fun."

He looked at me a second. A tiny painful look filled his eyes.

I slapped his arm. "I'm kidding. I know you guys would jump overboard to save me." I forced a laugh and Goldie smiled.

"We sure would—"

"As long as you were wearing every life jacket that was onboard." We both laughed this time.

With that, Goldie kissed my cheek, and confident that my friends were having a good cruise already (and deserved it), I headed back to my quarters.

I'd have to get to know Jackie better. She was, after all, my new roomie, and I'd be working with her very soon. Whatever had gone on with her and Betty, I had no idea, but I'd look into it, along with the overcharges—and the missing Remy Girard.

I eased the door to my cabin open very slowly so as not to wake Jackie. When I peeked inside, I saw her sitting on a chair, feet up on my bed, and painting her nails. Between each toe was a wad of cotton. Her hair was pulled up on her head and some orange cream covered her face.

Damn it all, but she still looked good.

"Oh, hi," I said coming in. She didn't move from my bed.

"Finding your way around?"

I nodded and watched while she painted the middle nail a deep bronze color. Goldie would love it. Jackie really didn't look at me as she spoke—more over my head—and I noticed she didn't address me by name. Guess she forgot it.

"Why, yes. I had a nice tour of the medical facility by Betty—"

Jackie groaned.

"—and Rico."

Jackie grinned.

Hmm. Very interesting. "I saw on the schedule that I'll be working with you on Monday."

She nodded. "That's fine. Read the manual so you know what the hell to do."

For a few seconds I stood there speechless. Jackie was an odd duck even if a pretty one. Her dark brown eyes and matching hair, even shoved up in a mess, emphasized her European features. If she were male, I'd call her swarthy, but since she wasn't, I had to go with exotic.

"Oh, yeah. I'll be sure to read the manual by then." I sat on her bed and shoved off my shoes. "There is one thing that will be very different for me, I'm sure."

"Hmm?"

"Well, I'm not used to dealing with the patients—"

"Passengers," she corrected without so much as a glance. Her right foot was up on my bed now, and she was gingerly painting the little toe with more care than she had acknowledged toward our conversation.

"Oh, yeah." I laughed. "I can't get used to calling them passengers. Anyway, I'm not used to charging them or having anything to do with that end of the care either. Billing is not my thing."

Her hand stopped. The nail-polish brush slipped. A bronze streak marked her upper foot. Suddenly I felt as if we'd docked in Paris. Jackie went on and on in French. The only words I understood were *diabolique* and *enfer*—both of which I guessed had something to do with hell. Either way, Jackie did not seem like a happy camper.

She had to be my ticket to solving this case and finding out who was taking all the money from overcharging passengers for medical care. Well, at least she could be a start. How convenient that she was rooming with me and—gulp—how *scary*.

Jackie swabbed off the nail polish from her skin. For a second, I thought I should just leave her alone. But then again, where better to start my questioning?

"So," I said, "We really don't need to deal with who gets charged how much?"

She seemed to have calmed herself as she pitched the bronze-covered swab into the trash. *"Oui."*

We what? I waited until it dawned on me that Jackie had slipped back into French. Hmm. Seems as if when she became upset, she would speak in her mother tongue. Speaking of mothers, I wish I had mine's ability to get the truth out of someone with just a look. "That's good. I'm not good with numbers." I laughed. So her story wasn't really any different from Betty's.

"Did I tell you that my family is on this cruise too?" I hoped that didn't sound as out of place and stupid as I felt saying it. I'd only had a minute amount of conversation with Jackie earlier, but there was a method to my madness.

"Family?"

"Yep. Parents and one uncle. Two friends too. Great friends. They're my roommates back home in Connecticut."

She didn't even look up.

"Whereabouts are you from, Jackie?"

She finished her toes, leaned back in the chair and let her feet stay on my bed until, I was guessing, her nails dried. *"Paree."*

Made me crave a croissant dripping in real butter and a black coffee—even though I'd prefer tea or decaf loaded with half and half. "Paris."

"I was born in New York City but raised in Paris since a baby."

So Jackie really was an American citizen. Actually she had dual citizenship. How cool. "Raised in Paris. Wow. Very glamorous."

"Do not let the world fool you." She gently took the cotton out from between her toes and then got up. When she stopped at the bathroom door and turned, she said, "Do not let *anyone* fool you. It could cost you."

My mouth dropped down to my knees, the usual sign that something had shocked the dickens out of me. Jagger very often was the cause, but Jackie's words added a bit more emotion, a new sensation stronger than anything Jagger had ever caused: fear.

The exotic woman with bronze toenails knew something.

That was all I could think about as I changed into a pair of silky black slacks and a silver-and-black sparkly sleeveless top and brushed my hair until it shone. Thank goodness Goldie had forced me to go shopping in the short time I'd had between receiving my assignment and sailing. There was no better personal shopper than my Gold. Even Miles would acknowledge that.

I took out my Estee Lauder perfume and sprayed my neck and wrists.

Jackie indeed was a piece of work to study, but right now I had to get ready for my "date" with Hunter. Date? Maybe I was being presumptuous. He probably didn't mean for it to be a date. Maybe he was just trying to welcome a new crewmember onboard.

When the knock sounded on my room's door, I stuck my feet into my black spike heels and gave myself one last look in the mirror before shoving the sink back up against the wall.

Hmm. Not bad.

Jackie had left sometime before supper, after telling me where and when to go eat with the crew. I had a nice turkey meal (not buffet) in the crewmembers' dining hall on deck two with Betty and the crew's purser, Claude Bernard, who now dated Jackie. Hmm. He told me that he handled all the crew paperwork and assisted in all crew matters. I already knew all that but didn't interrupt. I wondered how much he knew about me. I was anxious to meet the main medical receptionist, but never did, since I had to get back to my room to change.

Knock. Knock.

"Oops. Coming in a second!" One last look in

the mirror, and then I hurried and opened the door.

"Good evening."

Hunter Knight gave new meaning to the term "white knight in shining armor." He looked delicious. For a second I felt as if I'd traveled back in time to the *Love Boat* and he was the guest star of the show.

"Hey. Was I supposed to wear my uniform?"

He chuckled. "You look wonderful. When it is your time off, Pauline, you can wear whatever you like . . . or not."

The twinkle in his eye would be classified as X-rated.

And the thoughts on my mind would be too.

Hey, a girl needed a reprieve from fear/fraud/ and friends every once in a while.

Since it was my time off and Hunter's job involved planning fun for the passengers, we were allowed in the Bottlenose Lounge tonight. The chairs, a deep aquamarine, were shaped like half barrels with nautical designs of anchors on them.

On the walls were a series of golden dolphins that appeared to be swimming and jumping through waves. In the center of the place was a gigantic column-shaped tank of water—with three live dolphins swimming in it! At least they looked real. Less than four feet long, they must have been some kind of miniature, but it was really neat.

The column had to run two floors up, to the top deck, where they could go for air.

A band was set up on the stage, which was a few feet above the wooden dance floor. Tables of passengers filled the room and amid the chatter, the music played softly.

Hunter took my elbow and eased me toward the front of the room, where a bar, its glass top filled with colorful tiny fish, wrapped around the stage. He pointed to a stool shaped like a dolphin at the end. On the bar was a little gold "reserved" sign.

"Just for you, Pauline. Tonight is the welcome dance." He leaned near and whispered, "Welcome."

My toes curled in my pointy pumps.

The bartender came over. She nodded at Hunter and smiled at me. Hunter introduced her as Edie Edwards. She reminded me of Adele Girard, Fabio's receptionist and another of my friends, although dressed in her nice white crew's uniform, I was guessing that Edie wasn't an ex-con. Adele, however, was. "Nice to meet you," I said.

"Likewise, honey." Edie had a Southern accent similar to Goldie's. I wondered if she was from Louisiana too. Hunter excused himself to go talk to some passengers while Edie offered to get me a drink on Hunter's tab.

"Beer. Any kind," I said, liking her already. It was nice to see a woman as the bartender. She probably was better at listening and being sympathetic than any guy could be. Well, except maybe a gay one.

Edie laughed and poured me a mug from the tap. "So, you're the new nurse."

It wasn't a question, and I didn't remember Hunter mentioning it in our introduction. I had the feeling there was a tight-knit community of crewmembers onboard this ship. I only hoped that I could infiltrate it.

I took a sip of the ice-cold beer and smiled at Edie. She started to wipe the glass top of the bar with a white linen towel. "How long have you been working on this ship, Edie?"

She paused. "Too damn long." She chuckled.

I thought of Adele again. Edie could come across as motherly just as Adele had. I laughed along with her. "Well, I'm sorry the nurse that I replaced became . . . ill, but I'm glad to be here."

Edie's hand froze. "Yeah. Glad you are too."

That was the only insincere thing I'd heard her say yet.

"I hope it was nothing contagious." I watched her eyes and tried to remember if pupils constricted or dilated when someone was lying.

In the dim light I really couldn't tell, and besides, the light would affect her pupils. That much I knew from nursing head-injury patients.

She looked across the room, then started to

wipe again. "No. I don't think Remy, that was his name . . . *is* his name . . . Ha. I'm getting so tired tonight," she mumbled.

It wasn't even ten. If anyone should be dozing on her dolphin stool, it should have been me. In her profession, Edie had to be used to late nights. "I hope you're not getting whatever Remy had."

Her eyes widened. I could hear her gulp.

Suddenly I felt sorry for Edie, so I decided to change the subject. No sense in getting her angry with me. Besides, I already knew the truth about Remy. I might need Edie somewhere along the line. I looked out over the crowd.

Mostly twentysomethings dressed in sexy, short, tight outfits. More blondes than brunettes, and a few redheads, but all had long hair. The style, I guessed. The guys all looked delicious, but they were definitely outnumbered.

On the far wall sat a table of what looked like eligible bachelors. They were decked out in the same white tuxedos and varied in age. I guessed they must have been the male "hosts" Hunter had told me about. As I started to turn, I caught a glimpse of one with a bald head and started to smile. Until he turned around.

Uncle Walt!

Yikes! "Excuse me," I murmured and headed over to his table.

"Hey, Pauline. I'd love to dance with you, but I'm on duty," he said, smiling. "I got this gig at the last minute and they're going to rebate my fare. Seems the last old geezer croaked, and they hadn't had time to replace him. There are some women my age aboard, you know. They need attention that only I can give them."

I could only smile. There was no way I was going to scream, "What the hell are you doing at your age?" I couldn't. Not with the look of pride on his face. "You always luck out, don't you?"

My uncle nodded. "Your folks are already in bed, Pauline. Damn shame."

I grinned, then as I started to make more conversation, I heard a female voice behind me.

"I want him!"

"Abigail, you always get first pick. I want him. He's adorable in white."

Uncle Walt was now a lovely shade of crimson, smiling straight ahead. I turned to see two "mature" women arguing until one grabbed Uncle Walt's arm and said, "It's past your bedtime, Abigail. Don't wait up!"

With that, she and Uncle Walt were on the dance floor. And I laughed all the way back to my dolphin stool. Edie was now finishing someone's fancy drink.

"Seems the guys are outnumbered on this ship." I chuckled.

"What's new?" She looked up. "That's why Hunter hires those men. Escort the single women to dinner. Dance with them. You know. No sex though. All on the up and up, to give the women a good cruise to remember so they'll come back. We're always top-heavy with women on our cruises."

"Interesting job." I took another sip of beer and shifted on my dolphin. The back fin was the hard-surfaced lower back of the stool and it wasn't exactly a Lazy Boy.

She leaned forward. "I'll say, and on each cruise Hunter seems to come up with some doozies. If I were a few years younger! There's a few on this trip that I'd snag for myself."

We both laughed, and I was glad I'd gotten off the Remy interrogation—for now. I liked Edie.

A hand touched my shoulder. I swung around. "Oh, hi."

Hunter stood there, and I thought, *Hmm, I wouldn't mind snagging him.*

"Edie giving you the scoop on the ship?"

I nodded. "She's sweet."

"How about once around the dance floor?"

Thank goodness Miles and Goldie had given me some "speed dancing" lessons before embarking on this ship. It'd been some time since I'd danced in public, and yes, I'd worried that I'd make a fool of myself. I kept picturing Elaine from *Seinfeld*. "Sure."

Hunter took my hand and led me to the crowded floor. I realized it didn't matter if I had two left feet, since every passenger on this cruise seemed to be on the dance floor right now except my sleeping folks.

We eased into the middle of the crowd, where Hunter took me into his arms. Oh, my. Good thing it was so packed there, or my Jell-O legs might have me collapsing against his chest. Hmm. Looked like a pretty good cushion to break a fall.

The band played some kind of ballad. I looked around to see Goldie and Miles coming in the door and managed a weak wave since I didn't want to let go of Hunter's shoulders. He maneuvered me around the floor like an expert. "I'm guessing you've done this before," I said softly.

He chuckled against my cheek. "I could buy this ship if I had a nickel for every number I've danced to."

My lips curled. I really didn't want to think of him dancing with someone else.

He looked down at me. "It's part of my job, Pauline."

"Like the male hosts?" I tried to laugh, but it wouldn't come out.

"Not this time."

Yikes!

If I fell overboard right then, at least my body would keep warm from the delicious feeling floating throughout me.

We danced for several numbers, until I realized my feet hurt. Damn heels. But when I looked at how sexy all the other women looked in their shoes, I thought it was all worth the pain. However, I'd bet my next paycheck that none of the men even noticed one shoe.

A buzzing tickled my side.

Hunter looked down. "Seems I'm being paged." He looked at the number. "The captain. Could take a while."

"No problem. Duty calls." Great. Now I could sit.

"Let me get you a partner to finish the dance with." Before I could protest, Hunter waved to someone.

"It's really not necessary. I'll head back to my cabin—"

"Not alone. One of the crew will escort you. I have a new male host who isn't that busy yet."

"That's really not—"

"A gentleman does not leave his date stranded."

Not wanting to insult Hunter's chivalry, I smiled. "Thanks."

"Ah, here is the gentleman to fill in for me. Pauline. This is one of the newly hired escorts, Jay Smith."

Hunter's beeper sounded again. With a quick smile and peck on my cheek, he turned to leave.

"Nice to meet you, Pauline."

I swung around at the voice. "You? You? You!" I shut my eyes for a second. "An iceberg would be a welcome sight."

Five

"Open your eyes, Sherlock, or you'll bump into a passenger and knock them over."

"What the hell are *you* doing here, Jagger?" I opened my eyes in hopes that he'd be gone and it was all a mirage.

Then again, a mirage of Jagger would be the stuff fantasies were made of, not nightmares.

I could use a fantasy, now that Hunter was gone. I peeked out.

Jagger stood there in a white tux! Oh . . . my . . . God.

Before I opened my eyes fully, I said, "You're masquerading as a male host." It wasn't a question—more like a shocked statement.

"Let's not get into that."

I opened my eyes all the way. A male host! What a hoot! A few passengers were starting to stare at us where we stood in the middle of the dance floor. One young "kitten" wiggled up to Jagger and purred.

"Mr. Smith, you are naughty. You promised me the next dance." She eyed me up and down. "Who's *she*?"

Jagger grinned.

I wanted to smack kitty lady with a bag of catnip but instead said, "I'm only a crewmember, dear. You go ahead and dance with him. He's all yours." With that I hurried away to down my much-needed beer as I heard Jagger sputter something. Only thing I could make out was *dance*, *work* and something that sounded like *gritty*. I was going with "You look pretty."

I took the last sip of my beer and tried to catch Edie's attention to order another. I needed it. Damn. Jagger was like the clichéd bad penny. Hmm. Bad was right. I smiled to myself and turned toward the dance floor. It was so crowded I couldn't see him and kitty lady. Make that kitty girl. She had to be only twentysomething.

Damn. Made me feel old.

"What're you having, Sherlock?"

I swung around to see "Mr. Smith" standing there looking appetizing in his outfit. He didn't camouflage his face this time—thank goodness— as he'd done before on some cases. In the process, though, my arm caught on the dolphin's tail, and I stumbled forward—into his arms.

"Whoa. Whatever you're having, maybe you've had enough?" He pulled up a dolphin and sat next to me.

I straightened myself and held my head up with as much dignity as I had left. "I've only had one beer. You startled me. That's all." I had to keep talking louder and louder as the music increased in volume.

Jagger leaned near. I thought he was going to kiss me!

Stop it, Pauline. It is only because of the music.

"In your profession, Pauline, you have to get over someone sneaking up on you and not . . . fall off your fish."

I think he chuckled, which should have lightened the mood, but damn if he hadn't gotten so close that his hot breath tickled my ear. I had to take a few seconds to compose myself and think clearly. "It's just . . . Don't do that to me—that sneaking up thing—and I'll work on it." I couldn't say no one else would have caused that reaction.

Edie sidled over, a smile on her face. "Hey, good looking, what'll it be?"

"Another beer on tap, please," I said.

She looked at me. "I was talking to him, honey, but you got it." She smiled at Jagger while I tried to slink under my dolphin.

Jagger, obviously playing the gentleman host to a tee, said, "Scotch, neat, sweetie."

Made Edie's day with that one.

She went to get our drinks. "So, why are you really here? Did Fabio send you to—"

His Jagger-look said everything.

"Okay. Okay. No one tells you what to do. But really, why are you here?" I felt my eyes widen. "Oh, no! Don't tell me you have a case involved here too, and it's going to take precedence over mine, and you're going to need me to help! I'm not going to fall for *that* again. Don't even think—"

"I'm here for you, Sherlock. Strictly for *you*."

I told myself I should be insulted that Jagger came onboard to "save" my job and possibly me. I told myself I should politely thank him because surely I *could* use his help. Then I told myself I might not have been able to solve this medical-fraud case, since it now involved a missing Remy. In truth, I sure was thankful for Host Jay showing up.

"Gee, thanks." I took a sip of my beer as soon as Edie set it down.

"You two met before?" she asked.

We looked at each other. I had to let him take this one since I couldn't think fast enough to know if it mattered or not. I sure didn't want anyone suspecting us of being investigators.

Jagger sipped his Scotch, winked at Edie and said, "Nope. Pauline here just seems to be one of those women that you feel as if you've known all your life."

I sat there speechless.

But I also tucked that info into my brain and thought I had just learned more about how to lie with a straight face. Jagger was so damn good at that.

Jagger made polite conversation with Edie for a few minutes, and then, after we'd finished our drinks, made an excuse for us to leave—well, a reason for him to walk me back to my cabin.

He took me into an elevator I wasn't familiar with, and before I knew it, we were on the highest deck, looking out at the dark sea. With the lights from the *Golden Dolphin* casting golden shadows on the calm water and the moon's glow assisting, it looked like a Disneyland ride. One that Cinderella would have loved.

Soon little dolphin heads popped out of the top of the tank. Obviously the same guys who entertained the passengers down in the Bottlenose Lounge stared at us. I think the smaller of the three smiled at me.

"So, what have you found out so far?" he asked, ever so businesslike.

"Hmm?" I turned away from the dolphin tank. "Oh, yes, it is a nice night and fabulous view," I said, and then smiled.

Jagger looked as if he was in a hurry.

"What?" I said. "You have to get back and dance with some kit . . . with the ladies?"

"As a matter of fact, I do. So, make it snappy." He leaned against the railing, looking dangerous and in need of a Marlboro, even though he didn't smoke.

Not that I condoned smoking, but damn, he could do an ad any day of the week and apparently *any* time of the day. "Okay, here's what I have found out so far," I said, telling him about Jackie, Betty and missing Remy.

No reaction.

"Well? What do you think? Do you think his disappearance is related to my fraud case?"

He merely looked at me.

The look had me stop and think. Jagger was trying to teach me more about our profession—and damn it, but he could do it all with those dark eyes.

"Hmm. Okay, Remy went to school with my roommate Jackie, but that really doesn't tell us much unless . . . unless there was also something going on between them. But she's dating the crew's purser now. Betty said as much. Still, she and Remy could be in on . . . Wait." I looked Jagger in the eyes.

"We don't have enough to go on," I continued. "We have to find out Jackie and Remy's relationship, finances and if they were working together. I mean, how close could they have been if she's already dating Claude? Either Remy "disappeared" by choice with the dough or someone else is involved, maybe got greedy and conveniently did away with Remy Girard."

Nothing could compare to a Jagger smile that said, "Good job, Sherlock."

Since Jagger knew me so well, he said we should head back to my cabin, since it was late. Somewhere around eleven. Damn. He did know me way too well.

I was impressed with his sense of direction as he found my cabin without any wrong turns or having to ask for help. Maybe he'd been on this ship before. Nothing would surprise me. At least he had to have been around since it sailed, and maybe he scouted out the entire thing before running into me tonight. Again, sounded like something Jagger would do.

I looked at him. "When were you going to 'reveal' yourself to me?"

He chuckled, leaned over and opened the door.

I told myself it really didn't matter, as in the past, I had to convince myself it didn't matter whom Jagger worked for or what his other name was if he had one. I was getting used to the mystery of this guy.

"Fine. I guess I'll see you around. I'm going to have to orient myself to the infirmary a bit more tomorrow, even though I don't start until Monday.

Jackie is going to work with me then." I didn't tell him what a looker she was. Just her damn accent could get a guy hot.

"I'll be around." He leaned forward.

I gulped in preparation for a kiss, but he merely touched the pink (pepper spray) necklace that he'd given me and smiled. I fingered it myself after he let go. "Oh, yeah. Thanks for this. I'm sure I won't need it, but—" Jagger reached in and flipped on my light switch—and I let out a scream.

I muttered some more, but his hand over my lips muffled the sounds pretty good. I waved my hand to signal I'd be quiet if he let go. He did and I mumbled, "My . . . God."

Sprawled across the floor between our beds was Jackie—with a dolphin-handled knife sticking out of her back.

I thought I'd done a pretty good job of keeping my cool after we found Jackie's body. Now that the captain had been notified, and the security officer was here, doing an investigation, I sat staring at the carpet a few feet from Jackie's body. One plate-sized stain darkened the area.

"Here, drink this."

I looked up to see Jagger holding a glass of what I assumed was liquor.

I waved my hand. "I'm fine."

"That's why you've been sitting there staring at the carpet for an hour?"

I took the drink and downed it. I coughed until my brains shook and then my throat burned as if Strep had infected it, but in seconds, a warmth settled inside me. "An hour?" I whispered.

"You can't stay here."

I looked up to see Captain Duarte standing in the doorway. It wasn't just the uniform that gave him away. Nope. His demeanor said he was in charge around here. With dark hair, blue eyes and skin the bronzed gods would envy, the man standing there could be no one else but the captain of this ship.

Behind him was Claude Bernard. I wondered if he'd been questioned yet. He looked rather stoic. In all fairness, maybe the guy was in shock. He and Jackie hadn't been an item long, but it had to have affected him. Heck, I only knew her a few days and was devastated.

Guess anyone's death would cause those feelings.

"Ms. Sokol, arrangements have been made to move you from this cabin," the Captain said. "Since it is now a high-seas crime scene, and Ms. Arneau was also American, the FBI is on its way. You have to leave."

Gladly, I thought, *if I ever want to sleep again.*

"Unfortunately," he continued, "the only available space is a bit farther from the infirmary. We like our nurses close to it. In the morning we will do some juggling. For tonight, you can sleep in

Room 1112. With the full ship that we have, it is our only empty stateroom. The crew's purser, Mr. Bernard, will get you the key. He handles all the crew's needs and problems."

I already knew that and thought, *Great, I'd be close to Goldie and Miles*. Good. I could use them about now. Jagger leaned near and smiled.

I had already been questioned over and over by the captain and the safety officer from the ship sometime during my carpet-staring hour. "I'm guessing the FBI is going to want to talk to me too," I said to Jagger.

He nodded. "I understand they're being brought out by helicopter. Go to your new room and rest until they arrive. I'll get someone to help with your stuff after the FBI is done."

Yikes! I'm sure they were going to "go through" all my stuff too. Damn. At least I'd learned from my mother to keep all my clothes neat and clean at all times. One never knew when they'd become the source of an investigation. Of course that's not why my mother used to warn us to wear clean undies. Had more to do with getting into an accident and embarrassing her when the medical staff saw them.

I hoped the Feds would let me have my belongings soon, and I also hoped that Jagger wouldn't be the one moving my "unmentionables." But I didn't have the energy to argue right now.

Even though I'd been used to death and dying

in my nursing career, seeing Jackie's lifeless body was a whole different ball of wax. She was, after all, *murdered*. Only a few hours ago I'd been talking to her, watching her paint her nails. It all seemed so surreal now.

Who killed Jackie, and why?

Did the medical-insurance fraud have something to do with her death?

Was there a connection and, if so, what did that mean for my case . . . and my safety?

Jagger took my arm and guided me to the door. "Come on. I'll walk you to Deck Eleven."

In my numb state, I could barely feel his touch, but found it comforting. Once we were alone on the elevator, I said, "She had to have something to do with the fraud to be murdered."

"What do you have to go on?" He poked the button for Eleven.

Through the glass-enclosed back of the elevator, I watched the floors below becoming smaller and smaller. The purple and gold became a blur until the bell rang, indicating we were at our stop. Jagger held the door and stepped to the side so I could get out.

Thank goodness Claude had given Jagger the key. After he opened the door, I looked inside and gasped. "Wow. Nice place." All I wanted to do was collapse on the bed.

Too bad I can't enjoy it, I thought.

I sat on the stuffed beige chair near the bed and

shoved off my heels. In all the commotion, I'd forgotten how much my feet hurt. I would give anything to have my nightie to slip on right now. I felt so uncomfortable, all dressed up. But if the FBI arrived during the middle of the night to question me, I'd want to be properly dressed.

I looked up to see Jagger seated on the couch near the balcony. "You asked me something, but I've already forgotten what. Sorry."

He nodded. "I'm sure you're upset, Sherlock." His use of my nickname made me feel better. "I asked you what fact told you that Jackie was involved in the fraud, leading to her murder."

I stared at him a few seconds. "Nothing really, other than instinct." I waited for him to curl his lips or comment about not having facts, but right now I could care less about that reaction.

"And?"

Hmm. "Okay. And she was evasive about a few things, and just gave me the impression that she was involved in something. Besides, Remy went to school with her and maybe he's dead too."

"I trust your gut, Sherlock. Get to sleep, and we'll talk tomorrow."

I yawned. "Good plan. See you tomorrow." I looked at him and then at the door. "Please make sure the door locks on your way out."

He leaned back on the couch, lifting his feet over the end. "I'm not going out."

Gulp. As if I didn't have enough on my mind. Now Jagger was going to be here. I looked at him and normally would argue the point that I could take care of myself, but instead I said, "Thanks." With that, and after throwing a pillow and blanket to Jagger, I snuggled under the covers of the bed, clutching my pink necklace.

Maybe when I woke, this would all have been a bad dream.

Knock. Knock.

My eyelids fluttered open. Darkness surrounded me, along with a soft snoring. Jagger. I looked toward the door.

"Ms. Sokol, it is Captain Duarte. The FBI agents are here to talk to you."

Couldn't they wait until morning? I thought the ship's security officer had launched a very thorough start to the investigation, and had accepted my ironclad alibi.

"Ms. Sokol!" the captain's voice seemed less patient.

A murder onboard had to be a nightmare for him. I started to shove the covers off, but before I could, Jagger was up and standing at the door.

He opened it and said, "Easy does it. She's been through a lot."

I hugged my pillow and smiled. Then I threw off the covers and sat on the edge of the bed.

Good thing I had on my real clothes. Not too comfortable for sleeping, but modest enough to be questioned in despite the wrinkles.

The captain introduced me to several men, who asked all kinds of questions. They wore suits, and I figured if it were daytime they'd have on the clichéd sunglasses of the agents.

One was very tall with light hair, and probably would have a nice smile if he weren't so solemn. He was a looker. The other I barely noticed.

For a few seconds, I looked past them at the windows to see the sun peeking out over the horizon and longed for a cup of tea as I explained what little I knew about Jackie.

No, I hadn't seen her with anyone other than Betty and myself. I actually hadn't seen her out of the cabin. She never told me anything much except the little bit about Remy. The taller man, with blond hair, questioned me as if I were a suspect.

I had no motive other than she had painted her toenails on my bed, I wanted to shout. But I kept my cool despite my exhaustion, thinking I'd make myself look guilty if I got agitated.

You didn't want to appear on the wrong side of the law in front of the FBI. They made you feel guilty even when you weren't. At least, the blond J. Edgar Hoover did.

Finally they all left and Jagger looked at me. "How about some coffee?"

"I don't think they have a Dunkin Donuts on-board."

He smiled at the mention of "our" favorite coffee joint, and I realized I couldn't wait to get back to Hope Valley. Maybe I really was just a hometown kinda gal and never should have accepted this case on the high seas.

Especially since now a murder had been committed.

$\mathcal{S}$ix

Jagger handed me a steaming cup of hot tea where we sat in the coffee shop near the main lobby. They didn't have my usual hazelnut decaf, so Jagger made the correct decision to get me tea without even asking. I noticed the little paper label on the end of the string. Decaffeinated. Perfect. What a guy.

I didn't have to go on duty today, which was a blessing. Since we each got a day off every schedule, now I could concentrate on my case. But every time I saw some guy in a suit, my heart skipped a beat. I hoped they found out who killed Jackie soon, since it didn't feel too comfortable being a nurse on this ship. Hopefully, her murder had had nothing to do with being a nurse on The Golden Dolphin though. But it stuck in my mind.

One dead.

One missing.

I also didn't want my friends' and family's vacations to be ruined. Hopefully, they wouldn't find out about Jackie, but I doubted that the FBI wouldn't question everyone onboard.

Jagger sat down with his black coffee and handed me half a bagel with cream cheese and lox on it. I thanked him, slid the lox out and into my napkin when he turned around, then took a bite. Tasted a bit fishy but good, since I was starving. "Thanks."

He nodded. "So, what's your plan for today?"

I held the bagel near my lips. Jagger was asking me my plan. He was actually acting as if it were my case. I was in charge, and he was just here to help. I could tell *him* what to do now.

God willing.

"Well." I swallowed, took a sip of tea, winced since it was too hot and watched Jagger add more milk to it from the metal container on the table. I set down my bagel, because if I kept eating while he kept doing these things, these so-unlike-Jagger-type things, my jaw would drop in shock and any bagel bites would cascade out. I took a sip of tea and smiled. "Perfect."

"You have a perfect plan?"

"Er . . . yeah, but I meant the tea was perfect. Thanks."

He looked at me over his cup. "The plan?"

I set my cup down. "No, I don't have a detailed plan to relate to you. I just got here yesterday, got a short tour of the infirmary, met a few nurses and then my roommate was killed. Not a lot of free time in that scenario."

"Maybe you shouldn't have gone out dancing last night."

As soon as he said it, my eyes widened, and I could tell he wished he could suck back the words. Ha! Imagine Jagger wanting to take back what he said. I smiled inside so as not to make fun of him. "I'm always working, Jagger. Even when on the dance floor, I can scan the room, get information from the crew and bartender. Always on the job."

Even *I* didn't buy that.

Jagger merely gave me a look that said, "Yeah, right," but he kept his mouth shut and ate and drank in silence.

Several passengers walked by carrying their coffee and sweets. They sat at the glass tables next to us.

"As soon as I finish, I'm off to the infirmary."

He looked at me.

I moved my hand away from my hot tea so as not to knock over the cup when I said, "We. We are off to the infirmary."

"Atta girl, Sherlock."

"Hey, good looking, you come to snoop around?"

My eyes widened as I looked at Rico, who was working the nursing station today. How in the world did he know? My mouth went dry, and I couldn't think of a lie.

Jagger pushed me forward. " 'Good looking' is here to orient herself to the place before she has to start duty."

Rico glared at Jagger for a moment. "Ah, the male host."

I swallowed back a laugh. Apparently there *was* a very active crew's grapevine around here—and the enigmatic Jagger was the juiciest grape this cruise.

I eased past Jagger. "Yeah, Rico, I'm here to snoop around, as you say. I want to be very familiar with the place before Monday."

He smiled at me. I felt Jagger stiffen.

Yes! Obviously he'd noticed and didn't like what he'd seen.

"No problem," Rico said. "The place is empty. Just passed out a shitload of seasick pills. Other than that and a kitchen worker cutting his finger, the day is slow." He waved toward the examining/treatment room. Have at it."

When Jagger started to step forward, Rico stood. "Can I help you?"

Yikes! "Oh . . . him. Well, funny thing . . ." I looked toward Jagger for a life vest. Nothing. He left me drowning. "Seems as if we have a common friend back in the States—"

Rico laughed. "Pauline, we're near the coast of the U.S., not off in some foreign land."

I forced a laugh. Jagger remained silent, probably thinking Rico was a jerk. "True. But we just met . . . that is, Jag . . . um . . . Jay and I met at the dance, and I wanted to talk about our friend before he has to go back to work."

I wished I could get sucked out the porthole.

Thank goodness a woman came through the doorway holding a napkin to her bleeding nose. Not that I was glad she had a nosebleed, but it gave us the opportunity to hightail it away from Rico while he tended to the patient.

Jagger and I went into an exam room, where I started to open drawers and look in shelves, all the while making ridiculous conversation with "Jay" about our fictitious friend. I was actually learning the layout of the place. If I had to treat a patient, I wanted to know what to do and where things were.

While Rico cleaned up the area, Jagger and I eyed a small desk area that held a computer and notepads. A file cabinet, marked STAFF, sat on the side.

"Look at that," I whispered.

Jagger glanced toward Rico then over at the file cabinet. "Observant."

I smiled.

Several passengers came to the reception desk and suddenly, voices started to escalate. Apparently they were complaining about the ridiculous cost to treat their mother's nosebleed. Rico didn't sound all too pleasant—more as if he'd been through this routine way too many times.

Interesting.

"Can I help you?"

I swung around to see a woman standing inches from me and staring at both Jagger and me. She had on a uniform, so I knew she was staff. I should have worn mine too, except that whoever had packed up my stuff to move me had made a mess of everything. I was going with the tall, blond FBI guy, who looked as if he could care less about a woman's rumpled clothing. Thank goodness I found the wrinkle-free white shorts and navy tee shirt I now wore.

"Oh, hi. I'm Pauline Sokol, the new nurse." I held out my hand, but she didn't take it. The woman was nearly a foot taller than myself and had deep brunette hair that was piled on top of her head with a few sexy strands dripping down the sides of her perfect face.

Already I didn't like her.

"I'm Topaz Rivera. I work the front desk here." She stared at Jagger. "What the hell are you doing in here, Jay?" Her tone changed considerably, and she flashed what had to be fake eyelashes at him. How the hell did she know him?

I decided Topaz Rivera looked more like an exotic dancer than a receptionist. A receptionist? I needed to get to know her.

She slithered over to Jagger and whispered something in his ear.

"Topaz!" Rico shouted. "Get your butt over here!"

She winked at Jagger, curled her lips at me and cursed at Rico, but she did leave.

"Phew. Thought she'd never leave," Jagger said.

Jagger's eyes still looked in Topaz's direction, so I slapped his arm. "The case?"

"Hmm? Oh, I told her the story about our mutual friend back in the States. She's cool with it."

"Shut up." I turned toward the wall and rolled my eyes then looked back toward the reception desk. Soon fists might be flying. Rico got up and shut the door between us. Great. No one could or should hear us or see us snooping around, although I did want to hear what was going on out there if it involved billing.

"Perfect." Jagger lifted the key to the file cabinet from his hand and unlocked it.

My mother could do that. She could produce a Dagwood-sized sandwich while you sat in her kitchen and you never saw her lift a finger. All of a sudden, poof, the sandwich would be on your plate.

I shook my head and decided not to even ask. There were many things that were better off not asking about where Jagger was concerned (and my mother too).

We gave a look through the windows on the doors toward the front desk and then turned our attention to the files. Jagger had already pulled out two. Jackie's and Topaz's. "Remy's is already gone," he said, while I contemplated why he'd picked the exotic dancer/receptionist's.

After a few minutes, I realized any jealousy that involved me, Jagger and Topaz was unfounded. "She's been the receptionist here for three years. Same time that Jackie's been onboard."

"And?"

"And, you'll have to check your files to see when the overbilling was reported, and how far back it goes."

"It seems as if the passengers are none too happy with the rates charged around here. How can we tell if all the money is going to the ship or being skimmed off?"

"I'll send an email to Adele at the agency and see what she can find out."

We heard a crash and quickly stashed the files back in the cabinet. Suddenly, Rico flung the door open and wheeled in one of the crewmembers with an icepack to his cheek. Jagger grabbed my arm and we left.

Rico winked at me as we passed by. And Jagger's hand tightened.

Once we were safely out in the hallway and no one was around, Jagger finally let go. Damn.

* * *

I was paged to the main desk, only to find my room had been changed. No swanky suite anymore. I was moved back down to the crew's quarters only a few doors away from where I'd been with Jackie. The crew's purser, Claude Bernard, gave me my key and said I was rooming with another medical staff crewmember. I figured it would be Betty. That would be a welcome relief. Despite knowing I shouldn't talk ill of the dead, Betty was a heck of lot nicer than Jackie.

When I got to my new room and opened the door, I instantly knew my assumption was wrong. Where my original quarters had looked as if it had been whitewashed, this place was a den of black. Darkened curtains hung from the portholes. The bedspreads were red with black trim. If I didn't know any better, I'd assume the occupant of this place was practicing the oldest profession in the world, and I didn't mean being a nun.

I noticed my suitcase next to the bed by the bathroom door and figured I'd have to make the most of it.

If this continued the way it was going, I kinda hoped the ship would travel to another dimension in the Bermuda Triangle. Right now some paranormal Holiday Inn was sounding better and better.

I lifted my suitcase onto the bed and started to pull on the zipper.

The cabin door opened and before I could turn

around, I heard, "What the hell do you think you are doing here?"

Topaz stood in the doorway. I should have known. Who else would have "nautical brothel" décor?

"Oh, hi. I guess I'm rooming with you." I yanked the zipper until Topaz's hand covered mine.

"No chance in hell. Don't do a thing with that yet." She let go and grabbed the phone.

I stood silently listening to her talk to someone, and then another, and then finally heard her say, "Captain Duarte." Before I knew it, Purser Claude was at the door with another key for me.

"So sorry for the mix-up, Ms. Sokol. You will be in the cabin across from the infirmary."

"The one Jackie was killed in?" My mouth went dry. Damn. I felt sorry reminding him about it.

He hesitated. "No, the next one. Rooming with Betty Halfpenny."

Phew. "Perfect. Does she know? Because I'm getting kinda dizzy with all this moving around."

He chuckled. "Betty is on duty, but yes, she knows. You will enjoy rooming with her."

I looked at Topaz, who was now lying amongst the black and red.

"Well, it was nice," I joked and then grabbed my suitcases.

"Let me," Claude said.

Soon I was settled into Betty's cabin. As the senior crew nurse, she'd been bunking alone. I hated to impose, but Claude had said there was no problem with Betty, and I wouldn't be here that long anyway. He also had said to forgive Topaz, but she just had this "thing" about being alone.

Interesting.

The room was mostly done in white, but Betty had added some homey touches. A few frilly throw pillows, a tea service set on the dresser, and lacy off-white curtains over the portholes. It kind of had a British comfort, even though it still looked like a crew cabin.

Once unpacked, I flopped onto a bed and shut my eyes. I trusted this was the correct bed since the other had a hand-stitched yellow-and-red quilt neatly folded at the foot. Right now I couldn't care less if Betty bounded in and shoved me to the floor. Mentally I was wiped out, even though I had to get up soon and do more snooping.

I rolled to the side and picked up the phone. I left messages for Goldie, Miles, my uncle and parents, telling them of my new room. Apparently they were all out having a grand time. Good for them.

I got up and went to the bathroom to wash up and get my blood flowing. After a cool facial splashing, I felt invigorated. I would see what I could find out. Soon it would be lunchtime and maybe I'd learn more about the crew.

Remy would be first on my list now that Jackie was gone.

As much as I wanted to forget her, Topaz warranted looking into also. The woman was not very nice!

Of course that didn't make her a killer or someone who had committed fraud—but why didn't she want me in her room? What exactly was her "thing" about being alone?

I had a feeling it wasn't because she worried I might snore. Nope. Topaz Rivera seemed as if she were used to being alone. And how'd she manage that?

Her conversation with the captain did sound as if they were rather familiar. More fodder for my case. I took out the little pencil that I had gotten from Uncle Walt. He used it when he played golf so he could write down his scores. Then I took out my little spiral pad and jotted down all the notes I could about Topaz and Remy, and whatever else I thought was pertinent.

I stopped for a minute and tried to remember if Jackie still had on that woven friendship ankle bracelet (like the one Remy had worn) when I saw her body. Damn. I couldn't picture it. Had someone taken it off? And if so, why?

I went by the infirmary on my way out for lunch. Betty and Rico were sitting and playing Texas Hold 'em, a poker game I'd seen my nephews play before. "Hey, how's it going?"

Betty gave me a smile. I relaxed a little and started to believe what Purser Bernard had said, about her already knowing we were rooming together and that I'd enjoy it.

"He's royally kicking my arse," Betty said. She laughed. "I'm glad we'll be rooming together, Pauline. You've had a terrible welcome onboard."

I nodded and smiled. "Thanks. I was starting to feel very unwelcome indeed." We all chuckled and then I excused myself to go eat, feeling way better than I had a few minutes ago.

I intended to eat with the crew today but as I stepped on the elevator, I heard my mother's voice. "Well, it's about time you decided to join us, Pauline."

Mother was dressed in a yellow-and-green floral muumuu. She looked very Hawaiian despite her Polish features of a not so tiny nose and grayish eyes like mine.

Daddy had on white Bermuda shorts and a shirt that almost matched mother's outfit, except it had hibiscus on it where hers had bird of paradise.

They looked eerie and adorable all at the same time.

I swallowed back an explanation of my prior plans and decided to join them. "Where are you off to?"

"Not the buffet, Pauline," Mother said and stabbed at the main lobby button.

"Of course not. By the way, I just called you. I changed cabins." Suddenly I wondered if they knew about Jackie yet. Damn. They would be so worried. Of course I had no intention of bringing it up and wondered if the FBI really was going to question all the passengers. I figured they would, but it would take some time. I imagined they'd start with anyone who might be involved or knew Jackie.

"What was wrong with your cabin?" Daddy asked.

They didn't know. "Oh, something to do with the crew. I'm bunking with this adorable British woman, Betty."

Thank goodness the elevator opened to the lobby and we stepped out.

"Suga!"

I swung around to see Goldie and Miles hurrying toward us. All of a sudden, I felt as if I'd inhaled my mother's pine-scented Renuzit. A warm feeling, a feeling of family, friends and comfort, settled inside me. Obviously I needed to be with the gang for a few hours.

"Hey, guys!" I ran forward and hugged them.

Miles held me a second too long. "What's wrong?" he said.

I whispered, "I'll tell you later," and said much louder, "I really missed you two characters!"

Soon we were seated in the main dining room and ordering from the menu. I looked up to see

Goldie staring at me, concern in his big green eyes. If mother knew why I had switched rooms, her look would be similar—with an added order to get off the ship immediately.

I winked at him and watched him stab a forkful of his Caesar salad. Goldie had on navy slacks with a white nautical-print sweater. Gold braids dangled to his designer epaulets, and a navy knot hung against his chest. Tiny blue earrings, like little waves, swayed from his earlobes. The added touch was a navy-and-gold headband which held up auburn and golden curls around his head. Looked very "I Love Lucy," with a twenty-first-century chic.

I wondered who had more wigs, him or Dolly Parton.

My parents told us all about their "adventures," from bowling to swimming (which meant standing in the three-foot section of the pool) to dancing to an old band that they said sounded like Les Brown and His Orchestra. We all smiled at how they went on and on until mother yelled, "Yoo-hoo!" and waved at someone frantically.

I turned to look where she was waving.

Jagger stood in the doorway. A blonde was on his left, a brunette on his right, and trying to get into the scene was a redhead who could give Goldie a run for his money.

My Caesar salad rose in my throat.

* * *

Mother made small talk with Jagger about his being here and wasn't that nice, and I kept interrupting every time she started to say his real name. She scolded me and he excused himself. Probably more to get away from her and then to prevent her from blowing his cover.

"You really were rude, Pauline." She summoned the waiter. "Is everyone ready to order their lunch?"

"My salad is my lunch, Mother." I took another forkful and chewed.

"Nonsense. You need some protein."

If she started to get into my lack of calcium, I would politely get up and leave. We'd been through that in the past. Before I knew it, my mother was ordering a steak, medium rare, for me and one for herself. Goldie and Miles went with the pan-seared tuna, while Daddy ordered kielbasa and sauerkraut. It would never compare to my mother's though.

My mother fixed the same meal on each day of every week. Monday was meatloaf. Saturday was kielbasa and sauerkraut. How sweet that Daddy kept up the tradition when he could have had anything from prime rib to lobster.

"Could I speak to you a minute, Pauline?"

I turned to see Jagger standing above me.

Mother's eyes gleamed. "Why don't you join us, Mr. Jagger?"

Thank goodness he was alone and politely

managed to get out of the invitation with the excuse that he was working. I got up and followed him toward the bar. Near the corner, he turned and stopped. "Why did they move you?"

"Which time?" I laughed, but Jagger didn't.

I told him about playing "musical rooms," adding how I was so glad to be bunking with Betty instead of Topaz.

"Topaz . . . interesting," he said.

I tried to read his facial expression as to whether that meant she was a weirdo, as I thought, or that he was interested in her.

I went with the former, hoping to influence fate.

"Meet me after lunch on the deck where we were last night."

I started to ask for directions, but thought I'd sound stupid, so I just nodded. I had noticed the waiter passing out dishes at our table. "Fine. I better get back before my meal gets cold." Soon mother would be "yoo-hooing" me to come back. Before she made a scene, Jagger walked me over.

He held my arm very gently—only as if to guide me. Not any really good physical contact. When we got closer to the table, his grip tightened.

"Ouch!" I tried to swallow it back, but wasn't fast enough.

Everyone at the table stared at me. I was ready to turn to Jagger and ask what the hell he was doing, and then I looked down at my plate.

There sat a two-inch-thick rib eye steak smothered in sautéed mushrooms and onions. And standing at attention directly in the middle was a gold-handled dolphin knife.

Seven

Jagger caught me before I could run out, scream, or otherwise make a scene and scare my family, although his hold was anything but nonchalant. He leaned forward and whispered, "Take it easy, Sherlock."

My body relaxed—which turned out to be a mistake. Now I could feel his strong chest muscles and my mind flittered from a dead Jackie with a steak knife in her back to Jagger being the sexiest man onboard.

I pulled my thoughts to the present and told myself to cut it out. I was a professional investigator. Slowly I eased away from said chest and took my seat. My appetite was gone. How could I eat this steak when the knife was such a sad reminder . . . ?

After several minutes, Goldie leaned over. "If you don't want that, Miles and I'll split it." He said it softly, obviously so my mother couldn't hear.

I looked at the steak, the knife still in place. "Have at it."

"Is that Cary Grant over there?" Goldie shouted.

Mother turned and said, "I sure hope not, since the man has been dead for years."

I rolled my eyes, but at least Goldie was able to grab my plate and replace it with his. With a swiftness that had me gasp, he removed the knife, sliced the steak in two and stuck half on Miles's plate. Then he covered both with greens as camouflage.

I wiped my lips. "Um. That was delicious." Mother was so busy talking to Jagger now—God bless him for helping in the deception—she didn't pay any attention to me.

Soon we were all done and ready to head off in different directions.

"Maybe you can join us for dinner tonight, *Pączki*?" Daddy asked.

I kissed his cheek and hoped Jagger hadn't heard the nickname. Not that he hadn't before, but I wanted to be spared being called a fat donut in front of him yet again. "I may have to eat with the crew, Daddy. You enjoy yourselves though."

He winked at me. I smiled and thought it really was great that they were having such a good time away from Hope Valley. Mother was like a new woman. But her darn radar was still intact.

"I hope you get more protein with dinner, Pauline. Shame on you for not eating your steak."

I stood speechless while they got into the elevator on their way to go for a swim. Of course, they had to wait a few hours before getting into the water because Mother said they'd get cramps. As much as I tried to convince her that the old wives' tale wasn't true, she just ignored me. It really didn't pay to argue with Stella Sokol.

Goldie and Miles were going for a stroll, so I kissed each one on the cheek and turned around. No Jagger. No great surprise. I walked down the long hallway to the other set of elevators and headed to the upper deck to find him.

Jagger was never easy to find. Most times when we worked a case, the guy was incognito. But this trip, he had dressed like the male host he was hired to be. At lunch he'd worn white slacks and a striped short-sleeve shirt. Looked very yuppie/ cruise-like/yet macho. What a combo. I walked along the railing, ignoring the fact that if I slipped and fell through the rails, I would be a goner in the deep, dark ocean below. I'd be deep-sea dead for sure. Of course, even as a size four, I couldn't fit through the rails.

As I passed the tank that ran down to the Bottlenose Lounge, a little dolphin peeked its nose from the water, startling me.

I heard a chuckle and turned around to see Hunter standing there. "Cute. Isn't it?"

I looked at the dolphin. "Is it real? Really a

dolphin, that is? I mean, it's so much smaller than I would have expected."

"Buffeo dolphins are the smallest species. They don't get bigger than four feet. That's why we can keep them in this tank. Passengers get a kick out of them."

"They are neat-looking, but are they happy?" I wanted to lean over and pet the creature, but realized that if I fell in, the tank went all the way down to the Bottlenose Lounge. Suddenly I backed up a few feet. Talk about feeling claustrophobic. Guess these little guys were perfect, although the lounge was named after the bigger bottlenose species. Most people probably never heard of the buffeo.

Obviously Hunter noticed my unease, but had the good manners not to say anything. "They're sometimes called river dolphins since they are found in areas of the Amazon River."

"Hmm. Fresh water." I watched the three swimming around the pool while passengers stood and took pictures. A huge sign, DO NOT FEED THE DOLPHINS, was posted above the gold and purple decorated tank. "They are very graceful."

"Yeah. Hey, Pauline. Sorry about last night. How about a rain check?"

Suddenly the dolphins were not foremost on my mind. "Oh, sure."

"I'll give you a call later today, once I see how my schedule is going."

I nodded, and before I could say anything else, Hunter's cell phone rang and he excused himself. I gave one last look at the dolphins, smiled at the little clowns and turned around.

At the far end of the deck, near the bar and a pool shaped like—you guessed it—a dolphin, sat a gaggle of singles. All women. All scantily clad in colorful bikinis. I blew out a breath and looked past them for Jagger. At any second, I expected him to pop up behind me.

Nearing the gaggle, I heard a laugh—a Jagger laugh. The most buxom of the blondes bent down to brush her hand across her ankle, and then I saw my coworker.

Damn. Talk about a diamond in the rough.

He sat there talking and laughing with the group, but I knew that inside, he was aching to get away from the attention. I leaned against the nearest lounge chair and waited. Maybe I wouldn't rescue him for a few minutes.

How perfectly evil I felt.

Then he looked up and caught my eye. Oops. No way could I waste any more time with a look like *that* one. He and my mother were two pips when it came to conversing with their eyes. I hurried over and said, "I need to speak to you a moment."

He nodded. "Well, ladies, I'll be at the dance tonight."

Collectively they let out a big, pathetic, "Oooooooh." I shook my head and walked away from them, figuring Jagger would follow. I didn't want to see any more of swooning or who knew what else these chicks would do for attention. In my day, women didn't . . . oh . . . my . . . God.

I froze on the spot.

I'd become my *mother*.

I swallowed hard as if that would erase my thought and moved to a spot farther down the bar. "Anything you have on tap. Anything. And fast."

"Make that two," Jagger said from behind.

We got our beers and walked toward the bow of the ship. The wind made it difficult to maneuver, and occasionally I'd feel Jagger's hand on my back as if trying to keep me from getting blown overboard.

White puffy clouds dotted the sky and seemed to follow along as the ship moved. I could see the horizon a gazillion miles away and thought there was no way that the Bermuda Triangle was going to affect this ship.

A salty sea breeze made the beer taste all the better as we sat on two steps of the stairs that led up to a deck where passengers were not allowed. Occasionally I could hear the squeak of the dolphins and would smile to myself.

I took another sip and said, "Oh. Did you happen to notice if Jackie had on a rope ankle bracelet when we saw her . . . ? Her—"

"She didn't." He took a sip of his beer, looked out over the railings and said, "Why?"

It wasn't an accusatory tone. Thank goodness. My chest puffed up like a peacock's when I said, "Well, I remembered she had one on when she was painting her toes. And, in a photo she had under her pillow, Remy had one on his wrist. It looked the same."

Jagger sat silently for what seemed like hours. Slowly he turned to me and said, "Atta girl, Sherlock."

The wind could have blown me overboard, and I'd die happy.

At least Jagger and I had something that had to be relevant to the case. A rope bracelet or an anklet. He was going to share what we knew with the FBI agents, and I jotted down a note for myself. Not sure what would become of the information, I put a star next to it and decided we needed to get into the infirmary again.

Jagger had to go for an "appointment" with one of the female passengers, who apparently had requested him for a bowling game. *Yeah, right*, I thought to myself. Bowling, *shmowling*. I made my way back to my cabin to freshen up and then head off to the infirmary.

When I walked through the door of my room, Betty let out a gasp. She swung around and then relaxed. "Oh, my. I'm not used to having someone walk in on me."

She had been sitting in the chair reading. Not

like she was doing something illegal. But I understood. She was used to her privacy.

"I'm sorry. Next time I'll knock first."

"No need. You live here now. How's your day going?" She set her copy of what looked like some kind of cookbook down on the bed.

Betty would make a perfect homemaker, I thought. I sat on my bed. "Good. I'm doing well. Had a nice lunch with my family and friends."

Her eyebrows rose. "Oh. You didn't lunch with the crew?"

My eyes widened. "Was I supposed to?"

"No, Pauline. On your free time, you can do as you wish. Actually, Captain Duarte encourages the crew to socialize with the guests."

I thought of Jagger. Socialize, *shmocialize*. "Oh, hey, Betty, do you know why Topaz didn't want me rooming with her?"

A darkness filled Betty's eyes. Or at least that's how I read them. Then again, a cloud had passed over the sun and the porthole suddenly darkened. I wondered if I could get myself a book on reading body language.

"Well, knowing Topaz, she doesn't want anyone in her room. She's always been a loner since she took the job on this ship. And I'm guessing she just doesn't want anyone in her space." She leaned over and patted my arm. "Don't take it personally."

I smiled. "I won't. And thanks for letting me stay here."

She smiled back.

I wanted to ask about Jackie's anklet, but didn't know how to phrase it so that Betty wouldn't grow suspicious. She started to chatter on about cooking and the book she was reading until I thought I was wasting my time off and really needed to get to the infirmary.

I excused myself and went to freshen up and brush my teeth. Betty started to read again.

"I'm off to orient myself more. See you later."

She nodded politely without taking her eyes off the page. I'd bet she could whip up a mean kidney pie or fish and chips.

Several crewmembers were walking along the hallway as I stepped out of my room. Nothing suspicious going on. Through the glass doors, I could see Topaz sitting in the infirmary. Great. Now I'd have to deal with her while I tried to snoop around.

Next to her sat a nice-looking man in his forties, reading a magazine. There weren't any patients in the waiting room. A quiet day. Good—just the way I liked it.

Topaz looked up when I walked in. "What do you want?"

Yikes. What did I ever do to her? I told myself that she had a chip on her shoulder that had nothing to do with me. I'll bet she wanted to be a nurse and flunked out of school or something like that. Or maybe wanted to be blonde with pale skin. "Oh, hi, Topaz. I'm just going to continue my orientation before I start work here Monday."

The man looked up. He stood and held out a hand. "I'm Doctor VanHamon. Peter. You can call me Peter. You must be the . . . new nurse."

I shook his hand and thought he looked a bit flustered when he'd mentioned my being the new nurse. Guess having one missing and one dead could do that to you. I introduced myself and chatted for a few minutes with Peter, learning he took his vacation from his OB/GYN practice to work cruise ships for fun.

He came from Minneapolis with his family, who was allowed to come on the cruise too. His kids weren't in school yet, so it worked out. A free trip—as if a doctor needed that—although plenty of the docs I knew were penny-pinchers. But I liked him, and he said to make myself at home and that if I had any questions, he'd be around.

Topaz sat there filing her nails. Dark red nails today. She never said another word.

Suddenly the door swung open and a crewmember wheeled in a girl in a bikini. Apparently she'd fainted. My first thought was too much sun and too many piña coladas—or maybe I was showing my age and some fancy-named Martini with chocolate in it was to blame. The doctor and

Rico, who'd come out from the back room when the bell rang signaling someone had come in, took her to an exam room.

Topaz started to question one of the woman's friends and found out that she was the patient's sister. All I could hear was credit card and insurance information. I noted the order of the request and decided to hang around despite Topaz's occasional dirty looks.

"I don't want to disturb them," I whispered and motioned with my head toward the exam room. Guessing Topaz didn't send me out the door because the doctor had said I could look around, I sat near the reception desk and pretended to read Peter's copy of the *American Journal of Obstetrics and Gynecology*.

After three pages I told myself I was thrilled not be working OB anymore.

"Sign this," Topaz said to the sister.

She leaned over and began to read the form.

Topaz shoved the pen toward her. "Standard stuff, honey. Just sign."

The sister paused. "Force of habit. I'm a law student."

Topaz grunted but still held the pen forward. "Well, good for you, honey. We've been taking care of patients for years though, and not signing means I have to go in there and tell the doc to stop doing whatever he is doing for your sister—maybe even saving her life."

My jaw dropped. Saving her life? The girl looked fine, just a bit pale. Was that true about stopping the treatment? Somehow I couldn't tell if she was kidding, but Topaz sure seemed forceful.

And the sister signed away.

And I told myself I had to get ahold of a copy of that form.

Eight

Topaz busied herself with the forms while the girl who'd passed out was given an IV for a few hours. It seemed as if there were hundreds of pages the poor sister had to sign. Occasionally I'd hear Topaz explain, very briefly and in a hurried voice, that this form was for the insurance company and this one was so they wouldn't sue. She said the patient had to sign that one.

Sounded as if the forms for the insurance could be signed by the sister, but not the ones about suing.

I'd been in the medical field for many years and never had to ask someone to sign something so they wouldn't sue. Patient care came first. The lawsuit stuff was left up to the hospital attorneys. I always gave my best when it came to care, so I really didn't worry.

The sister begrudgingly signed so many forms she finally said, "I don't give a damn what they are for," wrote away and insisted she be let in to sit with her sister, whose color was now returning to her face.

I heard Rico say something about not eating all day and the sun. I concluded that a bit of alcohol had added to the problem. Guess she wanted her bikini to fit, he'd said then laughed.

While Topaz had her head down, reading, I winked at Rico, who grinned back, and then walked to the back of the next room and to the desk near the crew's files. It was the same place Jagger and I had been before. Since Rico didn't come by to throw me out, I parked myself in the chair. Suddenly, I remembered the file cabinet was locked. Jagger had magically produced the key, so I sat there trying to think like Jagger.

Ha!

Okay, thinking like Jagger proved to be a monumental task, so I tried to think like an investigator. Where would the staff keep the keys? They wouldn't want to take too long to find a chart of a staff member who was injured, so . . .

I started opening desk drawers. I searched the desktop. Normal stuff like pens, paper, notepads and a stapler. Then I leaned back and looked up. I spied a hook beneath the desktop.

"Bingo," I whispered.

In moments, I had opened the file cabinet and

started to look through the crew's files. Only a few names were familiar, so I began with them. Betty, of course, was the perfect example of good health, right down to all updated inoculations. However, there was a note about losing a few pounds. Yikes. I wasn't going to pass that information along to her.

I read through the captain's file, and then Hunter's, which had me blushing a few times when it came to the more personal health issues. Thank goodness he had no problems or communicable diseases. I tucked all the information into the part of my brain labeled "hunks"—it was already nearly full, and had been from the first time I'd met Jagger.

I looked much more closely through quiet and gentlemanly Claude Bernard's file. I had liked him from the first time I'd met him. I figured since he'd only been dating Jackie a few weeks, he might not know much about her death. Since he was still on the job, I supposed Claude must have had a very tight alibi. That's right: He really had been working at the time Jackie would have been killed.

At first I'd wondered if he might have killed her because he was jealous of Remy. Maybe he'd killed Remy too? It would makes sense that a jealous lover would do something like that if he were crazy.

Claude didn't seem crazy.

According to his chart, Claude was in darn good shape: perfect blood pressure, perfect cholesterol levels, and textbook lab results for all his other blood work. The guy had to work out, to look so good and be in such good physical health. I read through the rest of the pages, noting he was allergic to shellfish. Poor guy couldn't enjoy some of the extravagant buffets around here.

Topaz yelled something.

I looked up to see Rico hurrying to help with another patient, who was holding his arm. A possible fracture. Peter was examining him, so I returned to my snooping. Thank goodness I had the time to "orient" myself to this place.

On the inside cover of Claude's chart, I noticed a scribble in longhand. *Tricheur*. The handwriting looked distinctly female. Maybe Betty's, but she'd write in English. Then again, she could know several languages. I'd have to find that out. Maybe Claude was involved in the fraud scam too. Damn, there were so many suspects on a cruise ship. Folks came and went way too frequently.

I jotted down *tricheur* on my notepad to find out the meaning. I'd had Spanish in high school and didn't think the world looked Spanish. Hmm. Maybe . . . French.

Probably Jackie had written it.

* * *

After sticking Claude's chart back and thumbing through a few more, I leaned back, bored. I'd been there for over two hours, and Topaz hadn't come to throw me out yet. Wow. The exam room was empty. Guess the arm wasn't broken after all. Good. I didn't hear any arguments, so maybe the price seemed right for that guy—or he had no clue as to standard charges for the medical care he'd received.

I was going with that.

I leaned farther back and shoved my arms behind my head, shutting my eyes for a few seconds. If Hunter did call me, I'd be too damn tired to go out tonight.

I was getting old. Thirty-five on my last birthday. Yikes.

My eyes flew open. I couldn't go down that age-road right now, so I sat forward and, in the process, knocked the desk with my knee. "Ouch!" I bit back any more words as best I could while the side panel of the desk popped open a bit. Great. Now they'd deduct the cost of repairs from my salary. As I tried to shove it back into place, I told myself it didn't matter, since Fabio would owe me big time when I solved this case. Something kept the panel from catching. I stuck my fingers in the space and touched something. When I wiggled them, it fell out.

A manila folder.

Just like all the other crew's files. *Oh well*, I

thought, *it must have fallen through by mistake.* I picked it up to stick it in the file cabinet—then I saw the name on top.

Remy Girard.

Oh . . . my . . . God.

Within seconds, I had the file stuffed inside my shirt. I wiggled and jiggled until I was certain no one would notice. I stuck the key back on the hook, stood, made sure I looked normal and started to walk out. Topaz had her head in a magazine— thank goodness. I wasn't about to bother her. Rico sat at the reception area, typing something on a computer keyboard. He looked up.

My mouth went dry. I forced a smile accompanied by as friendly a wink as I could manage and hightailed it out of the reception area before anyone could say *boo*.

I was scared enough!

On the short distance to my cabin, I prayed to Saint Theresa that Betty would be out somewhere, and I added that I really wasn't stealing the chart. I had the full intention of returning it very soon, so any punishment for my sin should be put on hold to give me a chance.

What I would have loved to find out was, did it fall into the space between the panel and the desktop, or had someone hidden it there?

Maybe the contents of the file would answer that question.

* * *

"Afternoon, Pauline," Betty's cheerful voice said as I stumbled into the room. "Everything all right?" She chuckled. "Looks as if someone is chasing you!"

Damn. "Oh, hey." The folder poked into my chest, but I managed a laugh. "Probably a slew of good-looking single guys."

"Right-oh," she said.

Thank goodness Betty looked dressed to go out. She was off duty now, and I hoped and prayed she had a date or a meeting or something outside this damn tiny cabin. I couldn't even go into the loo to hide, since I'd surely have an attack of claustrophobia in the tiny space.

I sat on my bed and leaned forward, despite cardboard sticking into my skin, so that the chart wouldn't show. "Hunter told me all about those cute little dolphins."

Betty gave me an odd look. Well, her look wasn't really odd, more like she thought I was. And why shouldn't she? I *was* being weird, but better to look weird than guilty.

"Yes, they are darling fellows. They bathe so gracefully," she said.

I pictured the buffeo dolphin with little sponges and soap on a rope around what should be their necks, but then realized Betty meant swim. They swam gracefully. Jackie would have scoffed at her British expressions.

Jackie. I shut my eyes and said a quick prayer

for her. The way she'd treated Betty made me guess that Jackie didn't make friends very easily, and more than likely made enemies in seconds with a lash of her oh-so-very-glamorous accent.

I noticed Betty looking at me as if waiting for me to say something. "Oh, yeah. They are cuties, but that tank is so deep." Great. I sounded like a fool.

Betty must have agreed. She went to her closet and said, "I'm off for the afternoon. Some of the rooms can get so cold I need my jumper."

Jumper? Now I pictured Betty in a navy pinafore-type jumper, looking very schoolgirlish. She pulled a navy sweater from a hanger. Well, at least I had the color correct.

As soon as she closed the closet, I hurried to the bathroom and only partially closed the door because of my small-space anxiety. Didn't want to get caught if she came back. At least I could take the folder out without a problem. I'd bent it in half when I leaned forward, but I couldn't worry about that; since the contents were more important.

I listened for any noise and then went out. Betty must have gone off to wherever. There certainly were plenty of places onboard to spend your time off. I tucked my shirt back in and sat on the edge of my bed. Pulling the pillow close, I got ready to shove the file underneath if Betty came back suddenly.

Knock. Knock.

Damn! I shoved the file under the pillow. Wait a minute. Betty wouldn't knock. I stood up, made sure the file was covered and looked out the peephole. It was Jagger.

I opened the door yanked him in and said, "Geez. What timing."

He gave me an odd look.

"Sit down and look." I pulled the manila folder out from under the pillow and told him how I'd found it. "So, what do you think?"

He stared at it for a few seconds. "I won't know until we see what is inside."

My heart sank. I wanted praise for finding it! Then again, this was a job and I worked for pay, not Jagger's compliments. Still, they didn't hurt.

I opened the folder, feeling a bit as if I were violating Remy's privacy. Maybe because it wasn't for a medical reason—other than finding something out about my fraud case or why he went missing.

Jagger leaned forward. Damn. I had to take a deep breath and tell myself that Jagger pheromones did nothing to me. Ha! I swallowed, blew out a breath and looked at the folder.

"Hmm," I said after reading for a few minutes.

"Hmm what?" Jagger took out his standard toothpick, unwrapped it then stuck it into his mouth. He didn't smoke, that I knew of, but used the toothpick to help him think—I assumed. He certainly didn't seem like someone who would have a nervous habit.

"Well, sounds as if Remy might not have been too healthy."

"Oh?" Jagger tilted the folder so he could see it. "Blood pressure elevated. Hurt his ankle, bent his arm, cut his finger—all in a month's time. Maybe the guy was just accident prone."

I looked up. "You think so?"

"Do you?"

"You sound like a psychiatrist, parroting everything your patient says." I chuckled.

Jagger leaned closer. "Well?"

"Well . . . well, what?"

"Are you cured?"

Not from pheromone overdose.

Before I could ease away, Jagger moved forward even more. Soon his face was right next to mine and his lips . . . yep, were aiming for mine.

Emotionally and physically I wanted him to proceed. But my logical mind interfered, so I leaned back and said, "You think you can . . . you know—"

"Kiss you," he breathed.

Oh . . . my . . . God.

"Yeah. Yes. Randomly kiss me then go back to work as usual. Calling me Sherlock and pretending it never happened?"

For the first time since meeting Jagger, he

actually looked confused, and he even had me wondering what the hell I was doing.

"Sorry," he said.

Oh, damn. Now what could I say so I wouldn't sound like a fool? More of a fool, that is. "Er . . . we really should get this file back soon. And Betty may just pop back in any second."

File? *What file?* I thought. What is a file? We shouldn't be talking file.

Jagger looked at the folder on my lap. "Yeah."

If I could have fit through the porthole, I'd have been shark bait right then. No, being shark food would be too good of a way for me to die. I *had* wanted to kiss him, but something inside me said it wasn't right. Kissing could lead to . . . things. Things that would change our relationship forever. I mentally shook my head and said, "Let me see what kinds of workups and treatments Remy received."

Jagger pushed the folder toward me, brushing my knee, which I chose to ignore, and said, "Have at it, Sherlock."

I thumbed through the pages for several minutes. "Hmm. Oh." I turned the pages to see Remy had received four X-rays in the month of February. "Yikes. Wow." I noted that he'd been seen several more times and all kinds of blood work was done—all coming back normal.

Yet all being charged to the insurance company. "My, my."

Jagger yanked the file from my lap.

"What? What is wrong?" I said, startled.

"Yikes? Wow? My, my? What the hell are you reading to cause such orgasmic sounds?"

My mouth turned to Jell-O. No way could I respond to that question coming from Jagger.

"Well? Could he have been scamming the insurance company?"

I managed a nod.

"Perfect. All we have to do now is find out who he worked with—"

"And . . . and where he is," I squeaked out.

Now I knew why office romances are frowned upon.

Good thing I'd held my ground.

We went to the same café-style restaurant we'd eaten in earlier, and Jagger went to the counter to order. I sat myself down in a booth in the back. Several female singles had accosted us on the elevator, in the lobby and along the hallway. Host Jay seemed to be very popular.

I smiled to myself with pride, thinking of how I'd managed to get past Topaz to "return" Remy's file to its hiding place. Jagger had said he'd take care of reporting everything to "the authorities" (and made sure to take pictures of the file with his photo glasses). It was best to return it. I didn't even ask what authorities he meant or what he'd tell them about how I'd found the file.

I trusted Jagger with my life. I could trust him with a lie about me too.

I sat there watching the passengers come and go, getting lattés, herbal teas and bagels or muffins. Suddenly I realized I was hungry and wondered if Hunter had called me and left a message about dinner plans. I looked at my watch. Another hour to go before the crew's dining room opened.

"Thought you might want this."

Jagger set a hot tea down in front of me followed by a dish with half a bagel on it. Toasted. Cream cheese—and no lox.

His had the lox. I was embarrassed that he'd noticed how I'd hid them that morning, but what a guy.

"Thanks. I'm really not a fish person. I only like Boston scrod. White. Flaky. Not fishy-tasting. Plenty of bread crumbs and butter." I took a sip of tea and noticed Jagger shaking his head at me. That was his sign of exasperation. If he shook twice, I was in trouble.

"No need to go trawling for an excuse, Sherlock. You don't like lox. Fine. Next time tell me."

My face burned hotter than my tea.

"Trawling. As in fishing. Oh, I get it. Cute," I lied, and stuffed the bagel into my mouth.

"Okay, so far we have Remy disappearing and now a connection to the fraud. What next?"

I choked on my bagel.

Jagger jumped up and slammed me a good one on the back. "You all right?"

I nodded.

"Can you say something, to be sure?" I could see he was actually worried.

"Now is the time for all good men to come to the aid of their country. How's that?" My voice came out a bit scratchy, but that was because there had been a gigantic piece of bagel stuck in my throat. "I'm fine."

He nodded, took a sip of his black coffee and bit down on his bagel.

Then he shook his head again, but this time in a good way.

Nine

After our "coffee break," Jagger had to head off to work in the casino and I went back to my room. There was a message on the phone from Hunter. He couldn't meet me for dinner tonight, but would I come to the casino around eight and have a drink with him? He was supervising the bingo game.

Bingo.

Geez. My insides knotted. I'd had my fill of bingo on another case. But I called Hunter back and we were set for eight. I decided I'd rest awhile and then eat in the crew's dining room.

At the crewmembers' cafeteria, I realized I wasn't very hungry, but thought I might meet someone worthy of talking to and maybe learn more for my case.

I eased past a few chairs. The room was retro in design, looking very much like something out of the fifties—not that I was around in those days, but I'd seen TV shows, like *I Love Lucy* and *The Donna Reed Show*. Deep navy Formica tabletops sat on aluminum legs. Each table had red and white vinyl chairs with L-shaped legs, so you could bounce a little, and the floor was a checkerboard of black and white squares.

On all the walls, instead of the trusty dolphins, were old movie posters of stars like Marilyn Monroe, Cary Grant, Henry Fonda and even Arnold in his Terminator outfit. Either the designers had had a very nostalgic moment, or they wanted to give the crewmembers a break from the nautical motif.

I like this place a lot, I thought, as I went through the line, got a salad and perused the room for a place to sit.

"Hey, Peter, is anyone sitting here?" I found the doctor eating by himself.

He motioned for me to join him. I'd learned that he'd been on this particular trip about five times now, for all of his vacations from his practice. Not sure if he would be of any help, I decided I'd give it a shot. Besides, no one else in the room looked like they'd be any good to me right now.

At the far table, two of the FBI agents were drinking coffee and talking to several of the crew. I recognized a few of them as ones who lived along the same hallway as the infirmary. Hopefully, someone had seen something that would help get the murder solved. The blond FBI agent caught me looking at him, so I quickly turned my attention to Peter.

Peter looked at me. "Not too hungry?"

I glanced at my salad. "Late-afternoon snack has me quite satisfied." I felt myself smiling.

He grinned.

Geez! His mind had headed in the wrong direction! Before I turned pinker than the lox, I added, "Tea time. Couldn't resist a bagel. Those darn carbs sure can fill up a gal."

"Oh." He sounded disappointed.

"Where's your family?" I stabbed a piece of arugula and chewed on it.

He explained they were at the pool, and for some unknown reason, I gave him the details of the buffeo dolphins. He said his kids loved watching them, especially when they'd push a toy to the water's surface for their trainer.

"Yeah. That must be cute. Did you know that nurse—Remy Girard?"

Peter stared at me a few seconds. Okay, I could have used a better segue—or any segue, for that matter—but time was money—and maybe even life—here.

"I worked with him on several trips." He started to sip his Coke, all the time watching me over the rim of the can.

I nodded. "Then you did know him pretty well. I'm only curious, since I guess I'm the one replacing him. You know, they told me he was sick and left the ship. I figured the poor nurse must have been very ill to have to leave his job. Poor, poor thing." This time I blinked back fake tears and told myself I should get an Oscar. My lying and acting skills were getting much better as each case progressed.

Peter drank some more. I wondered if he wished there was rum in that Coke.

"Was he really sick?" I continued.

He looked around the room as if maybe trying to find someone to save him from me. "I . . . I never treated him for anything."

"No? Huh. He wasn't sick? Well, why did he just leave his job? I can't imagine that. It's such a wonderful job!"

"I really don't know why Remy left, Pauline. You'd have to ask . . ." He looked out across the room again.

I knew he was going to say *Jackie* but caught himself.

"Oh, Peter, I was also meaning to ask you, have you heard anything about . . . Jackie?"

His hands froze in midair.

I felt horrible, but told myself it was all part of the job. There were things in this business that I had to do, which were not pleasant but necessary.

"Heard?" Peter said.

"Yeah, heard anything else about her. I mean, I guess the cause of death was obviously stabbing, but anything else? She . . . she was my roommate, you know."

"No, I didn't. Nothing else in her chart of interest that I remember seeing. I already told the FBI all I knew."

How much did Peter know? And her chart? I wanted to ask where it was, but couldn't come up with a good reason I'd need to know and sure didn't want old Pete to be suspicious of me. "I noticed the FBI guys over there." We both looked in their direction. "I hope they find out something soon. Creeps me out that I could have been in the room . . . you know."

Peter touched my hand. "Don't worry. I'm sure it was an isolated case."

Isolated case? Hmm. How could old Pete be so sure?

"I hope they find her anklet."

He looked at me as if I were speaking French.

"She . . . lost it. Maybe it's in with her personal belongings. Brownish. Rope with some beads on it." I bit down on a giant piece of cucumber. Even *I* wanted to choke myself to shut up. But in my line of work I had to work every angle.

"Jackie's stuff is all packed up. The captain has it."

"Did you see the anklet?"

He shook his head, and then waved at someone behind me. I turned to see a woman carrying a toddler and a little girl walking alongside. "Adorable family," I said, and then excused myself.

As I stuck my tray on the conveyor belt, I wondered, *How can I break into the captain's office?*

My second thought was . . .

"You want to *what*?" Jagger said as I leaned over the craps table. He threw the dice.

"Two. Craps," the dealer called out.

Jagger glared at me while the man raked in Jagger's chips.

"Oops," I muttered.

This time when he shook his head, I knew I'd cost him a pretty penny. "I didn't think you were supposed to gamble while working."

He motioned toward the woman sitting next to him and whispered, "I *am* working." With that he pushed out another pile of chips. "And I don't know what the hell made me think you might bring me some good luck."

I blew out a breath while Jagger picked up the dice.

"I should just quit now, since you've probably contaminated my chance."

The woman next to him said, "Honey, do you want Madeline to blow for you?"

I didn't think she was talking dice.

The dealer looked impatient. Jagger shook his head and flung the dice.

"Lucky seven for the gentleman."

A pile of chips was pushed toward Jagger. "There," I whispered. "I feel much better now."

Jagger turned toward Madeline. She looked a few years older than myself and had no wedding ring on, but each finger had some kind of bauble that sparkled—and I wasn't thinking cubic zirconium.

The floral scent that hung in the air around her had to come from some expensive perfume. (Not that I knew expensive perfume. My only comparison was to the floral arrangements that decorated the caskets in Roosevelt's funeral parlor back home. Madeline did not smell like a funeral parlor.) The worst part about her, in my humble opinion, was her scratchy, sexy voice. Guys must love that.

"Maybe next time it won't take so long for you to win," Jagger said then handed her the pile of chips.

"Oh. Well, good. I'm glad for you," I said to her, grabbing Jagger's arm. "I need to talk to Jay here a minute."

She waved her hand as if dismissing a servant. "As long as you bring my *lucky* boy back." With that she set off into hysterics.

"Come on, lucky boy." We walked through the noisy casino until we were near the hallway to the elevators. Thank goodness the ship had some high-powered air-filtering system, because there was no scent of smoke hanging in the air. There was, however, the continuous *cling cling* of slot machines calling to the passengers, and the decorator had a change of mind and made the entire place silver and orange. No purple in sight.

Maybe silver and orange made passengers spend more money there.

Jagger led the way and before I knew it, we were on the upper deck, watching the dolphins frolicking in the tank. I bit my tongue before I ended up giving him an aquatic mammal lesson. I figured Jagger knew about the buffeo anyway.

He seemed to know everything else.

"What have you got so far?" he asked. One of the dolphins swam so close to the side of the tank, the water splashed Jagger's sleeve. He blinked and ignored it.

I chuckled and told him about my talk with Peter. "So, he really seemed as if he were keeping a secret. I don't know. He must know more about Remy than he lets on, but then again, all the darn staff seems to have some secret. They have this clandestine grapevine growing around here. Jackie's chart and personal belongings might be of help. They've already been moved from the infirmary. Too bad we didn't get to see them or her chart when we snooped around in there.

"I'm sure the FBI has read Jackie's chart over

and over and will probably take it when they leave the ship."

I rubbed the water beads from Jagger's sleeve and said, "That's why we need to see the chart tonight. We don't have to remove it from the room."

Jagger looked at me. I know he was about ready to remind me of how we'd gotten locked up together on other cases when we went snooping around.

Sometimes it wasn't such a bad deal.

I sucked in a breath as Jagger pushed me up against the wall and wrapped his arms around my waist. He leaned forward to kiss my lips, but there was no magic involved. He was doing it to fake out the crewmember walking down the hallway. The hallway that led to the captain's office.

The guy went past, grinning, and then Jagger moved away without a word.

All I could do was straighten my hairdo. I'd borrowed one of Goldie's black wigs and thought it looked pretty damn good with my fair complexion. Gave me a porcelain-doll appearance just short of Kabuki. At least that's how I looked at it. I'd also borrowed a royal blue sparkly top, and wore it over my black crepe slacks with my spike heels. The black ones with a diamond clip-on bow. Ouch, but sexy.

Looked damn good, even if in disguise.

Jagger had worn a black suit with a turtleneck.

Very Cary Grant/James Bond/lounge lizard. Very good-looking. He had a blond wig on that made him look a bit like Brad Pitt or Tab Hunter mixed with Beach Boy, depending on your age.

All in all, we'd managed not to look like ourselves. I had my mini camera that looked like a beeper in my evening purse along with Latex gloves, and I wore my pink necklace. Even with this evening attire, the necklace fit. Seemed it went with whatever I wore. Very chameleon-like—just like Jagger.

After our fake kiss (okay, my knees still buckled on contact), Jagger looked around and eased me closer to the office door. Since it was nighttime, the staff, along with the captain, was out socializing with the passengers. We'd passed through the Bottlenose Lounge on the way down here to make sure. The head honchos were there, along with the FBI guys.

Made me feel much better about our breaking and entering.

I looked down the hallway and then heard a click. When I turned back, Jagger was standing there with the door open! What a guy. Fake kisses and picking locks. Talk about talent.

In a few seconds we were inside. Jagger quietly shut the door and motioned for me to start looking on the other side of the room. As I slipped on my gloves, I figured I'd follow his lead and not talk.

After I searched through several piles of papers

on the sideboard, occasionally looking at Jagger, who was fishing through the stuff on the desk, he motioned for me to come over.

There in his hands was the manila folder that read JACQUELYN ARNEAU. The late Jackie.

Jagger slipped on his camera glasses. He started to click away, so I did the same with my "beeper." When he turned the page, a photo of what had to be Remy dropped to the floor followed by a cascade of several more.

I gasped.

"Quiet, Pauline."

As soon as he'd used my real name, I bit down on my lip and started to lift the pictures. Several were group photos of the crew. One even had Peter, Rico and Betty in it. The next was of Betty, Jackie and the man I assumed was Remy. All smiling into the camera as if they didn't have a care in the world. All were dressed alike, in their uniforms with white shorts that came to above their knees.

Remy was in the center with his arms around both women. When I saw Remy clearer now, I couldn't help but feel sorry for both him and Jackie. What had they gotten themselves into to cause her death and whatever had happened to him?

Fraud.

Money had to be the root of their problems.

Jagger nudged my arm. I looked at him and followed his gaze to the file.

Jackie had been given an advance on her paycheck a while back. The old records were still in her files. Hmm. She'd needed money. Maybe an advance in pay wasn't enough. So what else would she do to get it?

I looked up at Jagger. He winked at me. My knees wobbled. Delicious. I told myself to behave and get back to the matter at hand. Truthfully, it was getting easier and easier to ignore the tornadoes of maleness that flew off of Jagger. I was quite pleased that my professionalism had grown as I learned more and more about my job.

Jagger opened a bag that had Jackie's personal belongings inside. I recognized several things from our room, like her clock shaped like the Eiffel Tower, and her nail polish.

A tear escaped my eye. Before I could do anything about it, Jagger reached over and gently wiped the side of my face. Now I know what "swoon" meant. Damn, I could have melted into a puddle right then.

As good as I was about ignoring Jagger-maleness, being touched by him was still another matter.

But it was business as usual for Jagger. He pulled his hand away and motioned for me to look. In the bottom of the bag was a wallet. Jackie's, I guessed, although I'd never seen it. The wallet was light brown suede and, I figured, made in France. A big *J* was embossed on it. He opened it and lifted out her credit cards, six of them. Yikes. Then he pulled out her license and other cards we had no interest in. When he went to shut it, I touched his hand.

On the bottom part of the wallet was stitching. For some reason, it didn't look as if it belonged there. It wasn't a seam nor a fancy design. I pointed it out to Jagger. He ran his finger across the section and pushed down.

A tiny slit opened.

Jagger eased out a paper folded to the size of a stick of gum. With his gloves on, he carefully opened it.

In what I guessed was Jackie's handwriting was a list of numbers—with dollar amounts next to them. At the top she had written, "Owed."

On the bottom of the page, she had scribbled some notes in French. I wondered if Jagger knew what they meant. It wouldn't surprise me if he did. As a matter of fact, it looked like he was reading them and took a few pictures.

He refolded the paper, tucked it back into the secret compartment and had everything back in place before we heard it.

The *click* of the door.

Ten

Faster then the speed of light, Jagger put the room back in order, yanked me toward the balcony with a hand over my mouth—and soon we were in pitch darkness.

"I'm not going to scrweeeam," I whispered.

He held his hand in place.

Within seconds we were out on the balcony, which was a hundred times bigger than Goldie and Miles's. But below—way below—the waves clapped against the side of the ship, and my heart went into overtime.

Instead of a clear star-filled night, lightning flashed on the horizon, sprays of water moistened our faces, and the deep, dark water loomed below.

All my phobias crashed together, so I knew I'd die from fright before I hit the surface if I ever fell overboard. I was not a swimmer, nor was I able to float long enough to save my life. I freaked if I couldn't touch bottom. Besides, the giant waves below reminded me of *The Poseidon Adventure*. At any second, I half expected a gigantic wave to come from nowhere and flip the ship over.

Suddenly I wondered if Goldie had been correct. Was the Bermuda Triangle acting up?

Jagger pushed me closer to the edge and I could feel my body stiffen. I think he tried to whisper something in my ear, but if it wasn't something sexual or that we were going right back inside, I wanted nothing to do with whatever it was. I know he wanted us away from the French doors that led out there, but I didn't care.

I'd rather be found and thrown into the pokey than fall overboard.

"Move, Sherlock," he said firmly.

I shook my head, knowing full well that I couldn't take another step if I wanted to.

"Do you trust me?"

I nodded.

"Then move."

I shook my head again, although I really wanted to be able to talk and explain how I felt.

So, Jagger not being used to someone saying no, I found myself lifted up and moved away from the door. The problem was that in Jagger's arms I was now level with the top of the safety railing that kept the captain and his crew from falling overboard. One sneeze, and Jagger could let me go flying over the top.

I clamped onto his neck like superglue.

It took all of my control to ignore the fact that I could cause us *both* to fall into the sea.

I said a very fast prayer and before I knew it, I was set down over the railing to a very small ledge below. I think I blacked out. Maybe that's when he pried my hands off of him.

Within seconds, I found myself grabbing onto the closest part of the ship that I could reach (the damn railing), hoping it would keep me from heading down to Davy Jones's locker. I peeked over to see the waves far below and was glad, in one way, since they couldn't wash over me, but in another way, I was terrified that it was a darn long way to fall.

Soon Jagger was at my side, holding on to me and motioning for me to stay still—as if I wanted to Polka right here on this tiny ledge to the tune of "By the Beautiful Sea."

If the Bermuda Triangle didn't suck us into the surf, I might just jump, since I didn't think we could ever get off of there alive.

The fear factor was killing me.

My heart thudded. In the room, shadows moved along the wall. Doors opened and shut. We heard voices—muffled voices.

The lights popped on.

"Cleaning people," Jagger whispered.

Cleaning people? What the heck was he talking about? I thought he'd lost his mind. Maybe Jagger was more afraid than me. Naw. "Whaaaaaaaat?" I asked.

Who cared if I sounded like a frightened kid facing the Headless Horseman on Halloween?

"There are cleaning people in the office. When they're done, we can go back.... What is it, Sherlock?"

Frozen, I couldn't respond. The ship had tilted to one side. I didn't know or care if it was port or starboard. For me it was *hell*.

"You don't like water."

At least he didn't say I was scared shitless. I nodded and in seconds, Jagger's strong hold had me feeling a bit safer. Of course I wished that hold was on land or at least back in the safety of the hallway, so that I could enjoy it.

After what seemed like hours, Jagger's grip tightened. "The lights went out. I'm going to lift you over the railing back to the balcony. Remember, you said you trust me."

"Um." If I were watching us in a video, I'd probably laugh. My body had stiffened to near rigor mortis, and nothing—not even Jagger's kind words, sexy words or, finally, annoyed words—could loosen my muscles. So, with me like a surfboard, he tried to push my rigid body over the rail. But before he could, the boat shifted again. He stumbled but caught himself, causing me to grab out—and yank a tuft of hair from his head.

"Ouch!" he shouted as he instinctively reached up to his hair and let me go.

I slipped back to the deck—and Jagger stumbled backward off the small ledge.

I screamed.

He yelled.

I scrambled to my feet.

And suddenly his hands were clutching the ledge where I was standing.

His hands!

I could only see his hands!

"Sherlock! Sherrrrrrlock!"

Jagger could—no, would—fall to his death if I let my fears keep me safely on the ledge. Without thinking (since thinking would surely get me into trouble), I climbed back over the railing onto the balcony to keep the barrier between us for safety. I reached through the bars and grabbed his hands. "I've . . . got . . . you."

"Pull!"

I pulled. My damp hands flew back toward me, empty. "No!"

I stared for a few seconds then leaned forward.

His hands reached over the ledge again. "I'm standing on a pipe below."

The wind nearly snatched away his words, but I heard the wonderful sound and thanked God. "Try again." We repeated the action twice more and both times his wet grip slipped from mine, and on the first try one spike heel went overboard.

This last time I screamed, not caring if the cleaning people found us.

"Pauline. Help." His voice grew fainter.

Jagger was losing strength.

"I'm going to help!" With that I pulled with the strength adrenaline gives a mother whose child is pinned under a car. I yanked on his hands and arms and kept pressure on my hold with my leg wrapped around the railing until he was safely on top of the small ledge.

He lay there for a few minutes. Even fearless Jagger had to have lost a few years after that scene.

Once he was over the railing onto the large balcony, he clutched me in his arms. When his lips touched mine, I knew this was not just a "hey, thanks a lot" kinda kiss.

Yum.

After a quick trip back to my room to "touch up" my makeup, put on some dry clothes and grab a full pair of shoes, I was down in the casino at fifteen past eight.

"Suga!"

I swung around to see Goldie and Miles walking toward me. I couldn't help myself. I ran up to them and grabbed each in a bear hug.

Miles pushed me back to look at me. "Whoa. What's that all about? You all right?"

How could I tell my two best friends that I'd come so close to dying?

"Yes and no, I'm not. I need a drink."

Miles gasped.

Goldie swooned.

And Jagger walked up to me with a glass of something liquid and golden. "Drink it all—"

I snatched the shot glass from Jagger's hand and chugged the liquid down in one hot, choking swallow. "Arrgh!"

He shook his head. "—slowly. I was going to say drink it slowly."

"Now . . . you . . . tell me." My voice sounded as if I'd smoked a pack a day from birth.

Goldie reached over, his hand covered in a white silken glove that ran up to his elbow, and patted me on the back. "Suga. Suga. What caused all this?"

I looked around. Hunter was on the other side of the room with a group of passengers. He noticed me and gave me a wave along with an "I'll be over as soon as I can get away from this group" look.

I smiled as best I could after the choking incident (by the way, my throat still burned), waved and mouthed, "Take your time."

I motioned for Miles and Goldie to follow me to a secluded table in the back of the room. Behind the dolphin, whale and seahorse slot machines, we found an unoccupied table. I flopped into a chair, thinking whatever golden liquid Jagger had given me had me relaxed enough for a siesta. Only thing was, it was nearly bedtime.

Good old Gold patted me on the arm this time. "Tell us, Suga."

I looked at his ivory silk suit, flared pants, diamond necklace that matched gold dangling dolphin earrings with little emerald eyes (which I was certain Miles had bought for him) and tonight's wig choice—platinum blonde bob, classic Carol Channing. I told them the entire story.

But first I started with, "No screeching. Promise?"

They looked at each other. Grabbed each other's hand. And both nodded. I began and finished about tonight's event and Jackie's death with the two of them covering their mouths with their hands, eyes bulging, and blinking.

"Good boys," I said. "Anyway, no need to fret. Jagger and I are all right. Only lost one shoe."

Goldie gasped.

I wasn't sure if it was because I'd come so close to joining that shoe in the deep sea of death, or if the gasp was for the fact that I'd lost one of the only pair of sexy spike heels I owned—Prada, no less—and Goldie had picked them out for me during a huge sale.

I'm sure it was the first reason, but had to smile to myself about the last. "So now I have to find out more about—"

"Ah, Pauline, here you are. Hiding in the shadows with your . . . friends." Hunter gave them a curious look. Guess he was wondering if Goldie was Miles's girl. Ha!

"Oh, hey. Sorry I was late." I introduced everyone and soon Hunter had us at a private table playing blackjack.

I was losing my shirt.

Miles kept trying to give me signals when to hold and when to take another card, but I wasn't really able to fully concentrate. Had to be that golden stuff.

The dealer kept raking a card on the table in front of me, obviously so I'd bet faster, which made me all the more confused and a bit nervous.

"Damn. Okay. Hit me."

Miles and Goldie both groaned.

The dealer dealt me a card.

"Twenty-one," Jagger said, coming up from behind.

I recounted the cards. He was correct. We watched the dealer, who ended up with twenty-two, then shoved a pile of chips toward me.

Jagger seated himself to my left. "Guess *I* bring good luck."

My spine tingled. Hunter had been called away for a few minutes—and I kinda hoped he wouldn't return.

Now I was really getting confused.

After a few hands, and my losing three in a

row, Hunter touched my shoulder. "Ah. Seems as if my date needs some good luck from me."

I felt Jagger stiffen next to me.

And I smiled inside.

Then I wondered if he was getting up to leave, but looked to see him pointing for the dealer to hit him. Should be an interesting night, and I didn't mean the gambling.

My bad night turned worse when I heard, "Yoo-hoo, Pauline!"

Not wanting to waste any more of my hard-earned cash, I got up from my seat to see my parents heading over, Mother waving a white linen hanky as if surrendering.

"Oh, no," I mumbled, as with horror, I watched my parents take a spot near the table to watch the card game.

Hunter put his arm around my back as Jagger said, "She means well," and patted my hand.

Yikes. The two of them were vying for my attention—and I didn't mean the two of my parents. Having two gorgeous guys interested made me feel, excited, happy and scared, all rolled into one.

Damn. What a great feeling!

Goldie and Miles watched with pride and a bit of protectiveness, as Jagger and Hunter became the only two left with blackjack hands at our table.

I stood between them.

Every once in a while I'd look at Goldie and wink. He'd wink back. My mother kept going on and on about her and Daddy bowling today, and did I know that she had a strike?

"No, Mom. That's neat. Congrats."

"And, Pauline, your uncle is having the time of his life."

Daddy grunted. "Male host."

I smiled. *You dog, you, Uncle Walt.* "Glad it's keeping him busy. Does he even see his friend Mrs. Kolinsky?"

Like the nuns used to do in Catholic grammar school, Mother tucked the hanky into the sleeve of her sparkly robin's-egg blue dress. Goldie must have helped her pick it out. "No. She hooked up with a gang of women, and they are apparently having a ball too."

Did Mother just say, "Hooked up?" I couldn't speak for a few seconds. The air out at sea surely didn't have enough oxygen in it for senior citizens.

Finally I said, "Oh. That's great. I'm so glad you are all having such a good—"

"When are you going to start having a good time and stop working?" Mother asked, or make that *nagged*. "You have a choice between Mr. Jagger and that nice Mr. Hunter."

"Mom, I'm having a ball." I refused to discuss specifics, and I refused to explain that I hadn't even started my nursing job here yet, but had been working my case all this time. I shut my eyes, and suddenly the deep dark sea floated below. My eyelids flew open, and I grabbed on to the nearest thing I could—my mother's arm.

"What? What is wrong with you? You're in some kind of trouble with that darn job. Aren't you, Pauline Sokol?"

Yikes. When she used my surname, I *was* in trouble. With *her*. I let go. "Mom," I looked back and forth to see that Jagger and Hunter each had a pile of chips in front of them—of equal size. Wow. I'd missed the rivalry hand. "Mom, I'm not in trouble. I have to work on Monday, so I'm having fun today and tomorrow."

For several minutes I stood and watched Jagger and Hunter wheeling and dealing until Jagger's pile had three more chips than Hunter's.

Whoa boy.

Eleven

Betty flew up from being snuggled in her bed when I opened the door. "Oh. I'm so sorry," I whispered, although she was fully awake. I guessed she still wasn't used to having a roommate.

She waved a hand at me and flopped back down. "How are you doing?"

Not really in the mood for a conversation, but telling myself that I was working 24/7 and maybe something Betty would say might help my case, I sat on the chair by my bed, flung off my shoes and said, "I'm doing." I couldn't tell her about nearly falling off the ship tonight, so instead I told her about the card game—and how Hunter and one of the "hosts" duked it out until the end.

"Hunter lost that much? Golly. I'd hate to be the guy who beat him. Hunter hates to lose."

"Ha. Most men do."

Betty looked over my head as if in thought. I almost turned around to see if something or someone was behind me.

"Right-oh. Most men surely do." She pulled the covers over her shoulders.

"I'll let you get some sleep. Sorry I woke you. You working the morning shift?"

"I am." She yawned.

I wanted to tell her about Jackie's stuff and ask her what else she knew about Remy. I didn't want Betty annoyed with me though. If someone kept me awake, I had the tendency to get a bit grouchy. But Betty was so very proper and British, I decided I'd go for it. "Oh, hey, Betty."

"Um?"

I had no idea what to ask her and didn't want to lose the window of opportunity before she nodded off, so I came right out with, "What do you think happened to Remy Girard?"

If I thought others had looked at me oddly over the last few days, Betty had just outdone all of them. Now I felt like a fool. Why on earth would I come out with a question about Remy?

I had to work on my segues.

While she kept staring at me, I clarified, or at least tried to, with, "The reason I asked out of the blue like this is that I saw a man at the casino that kinda looked like him."

Betty pulled the covers higher. I couldn't see her face and didn't want to see the look of disgust and annoyance she probably was giving me—proper British or not.

"You think you saw Remy Girard?"

"Oh—" I laughed. "Oh, no. I know it wasn't him, he just reminded me of him."

"How do you know what he looked like?"

Yikes. Betty was a bit like the FBI making me feel guilty for no reason, as if I was the one being questioned here instead of the other way around. "Oh, well, one time Jackie—" I paused for a moment then finished with, "—showed me a picture. She had it under her pillow. I understand they were dating."

"Jackie didn't have relationships. She merely slept around to please herself. She never cared about anyone else except Jackie."

Harsh words for the dead!

There had to be something going on between Jackie and Betty. But if it were something like Betty being jealous, that didn't help me with Jackie maybe being involved in medical-insurance fraud.

"I have to tell you, Betty, Jackie didn't really welcome me aboard. I wonder if she didn't have a very good life back home."

Betty looked at me, shut her eyes and remained silent.

Great. She must have fallen asleep. I sat there a few seconds, not knowing what to do. Talk and wake her or let her go and get some sleep myself.

I went with the last thought and got up to go get undressed in the bathroom.

Before I made it to the door, Betty said, "Poor girl. Her mother left her father and two sisters when Jackie was only eleven. The other girls were much older, able to make lives for themselves. Jackie's father spent more time at the local pub than at their flat. She practically had to raise herself—and didn't do that great of a job, I might add."

The night was catching up to me, not to mention the golden liquid's effects on my brain, so I leaned against the wall and said, "I could see why. Poor thing."

Betty hadn't gotten up. She actually remained tucked in with her eyes shut. Odd, but at least she was giving me some info on Jackie. Now that I knew her background and that she'd gotten that advance on her paycheck, Jackie went to the head of the line for fraud suspicion.

Betty continued, "At least she made it through nursing school—"

"With Remy," I added, but Betty opened one eye and gave me a look of "what the hell does that have to do with anything?"

"But as far as she's . . . she had told me, her life was beastly and that's why she worked on ships. Not close to her sisters. No land connections really. No permanent home. No one to care or worry about . . . her."

"How about you, Betty? Do you have a land connection?"

"Me mum and three sisters live in London. My life started out quite different than how it came to be. Nurses are poorly paid, so I joined the cruise line and . . . well, I really love it. So I've stayed. I especially like the *Golden Dolphin*. Most of the crew speaks English—which isn't always the case, and the captain is a decent bloke. That makes a huge difference. If something doesn't go right, he works it out. He's not all mouth and trousers like some are."

Mouth? Trousers? Was she talking anatomy, wardrobe or about the captain? I stood, silent, not knowing what to say.

"Oh—" She shut her eyes, turned toward the wall and said, "All talk and no action."

I smiled. "Yeah. I knew that was what you meant," I lied, but Betty must have already dozed off. I wasn't that good a liar anyway.

When I finally woke and looked over at Betty's bed, it was empty and very neatly made. That reminded me that Sunday was my last free day, so I turned over and fell back to sleep.

After waking at nearly ten, I got up, showered, dressed and spent the day with my family.

Turned out to be the longest day of the trip.

But it came and went without incident—and,

unfortunately without progress on my case. I noticed Jagger and Uncle Walt around the ship several times with their "dates." Despite the dirty
looks given to me from the singles around Jagger,
I managed to pull him aside and fill him in on
what I found out about Jackie.

It was then he remembered to tell me what the
French writing in her chart said. *Cheater*. Hmm.
Was she referring to a lover? A friend? Remy?
Claude?

In French, Jackie actually had written about how
much money "they" were clearing from scamming the insurance companies by overcharging
the patients and pocketing the difference. It really
wasn't an earth-shattering discovery, but a solid
lead.

Bingo!

What we now needed to find out was, who was
working with Jackie, and did he kill her, since our
only suspect was now dead?

I emailed Fabio about the progress I'd made
with a wee little lie that the case would wrap up
soon. I left out the part about how Jackie's murder
left us with no live suspects.

Technicalities.

At least that's what I told myself as the ship
sailed through the finally calm waters on our way
to Miami. We were to dock there tomorrow for
part of the day and then head off to Bermuda. I

·was excited about seeing the island as I slathered SPF 45 sunblock on my fair skin.

Most of the afternoon I'd stayed on the upper deck, making friends with the dolphins, whom I had named Johnny, Jake and Gilbert. Johnny, after—you guessed it—Johnny Depp, my favorite actor.

Gilbert seemed to love to splash me, but I think we bonded. Made me miss my little Spanky all the more, although I knew he was in good hands with Miles's friends Chucky and Bernard. They would be wonderful foster "parents" to Spanky.

Johnny, or maybe Jake (those two looked like twins but I wasn't sure if there were such creatures as twin dolphins) poked his nose at Gilbert and they torpedoed down into the tank. I'll bet they gave the passengers in the Bottlenose Lounge a great show. The little aquatic clowns.

I gained nothing new at any meals, and since I had to work tomorrow, I headed off to sleep early. Betty had a date with one of the crew's security officers. Good-looking guy from England. I thought they made a perfect couple and told her so before I went to sleep—all alone.

At least I looked damn good in my white uniform compared to the stinking scrubs I usually had to wear when I got shanghaied back into my old nursing career—usually on Jagger's behalf.

I leaned closer to the mirror to make sure my makeup (a Goldie special complete with lessons on how to apply) and hair looked decent. When I leaned back, I said, "Good to go." With that I headed out of the cabin to the crew's dining hall for breakfast. I only had a half hour before work, so not much time to do my investigative work if the opportunity arose.

After a wonderful breakfast—buffet style—I walked to the infirmary, making sure I never told my mother about the spread of germs I probably just ate. I figured the staff were better at washing their hands and not touching food they didn't take than the passengers—or at least I hoped they were.

Topaz, sitting at the infirmiry reception desk, gave me a slight smile, a mumble and a nod.

"Hey, Topaz. Good morning."

She looked up. I got ready to hear some snide remark or maybe no remark at all. Not sure why she seemed to instantly dislike me, I gave her my best smile. "I'm looking forward to working with you"—then I decided to pull out all the stops and use some psychology on the woman with black nails and matching eye shadow. " I was thinking I'm so glad that you've been here awhile and can really show me the ropes."

Her dark eyes lightened.

Thank goodness she didn't ask how I knew she'd been there awhile. I made that part up as I aimed toward a congenial working relationship. "I'm excited about this different kind of nursing, and really glad you're here." With that, I remained silent and let all the gooey honey I'd just spewed out soak in.

She stood up and waved a hand for me to follow. Not certain if this was good or bad, I said a speed-dial prayer to Saint T and followed like an obedient child, keeping my wits about me in case she had something harmful in mind.

Maybe she was in on the fraud and had even killed Jackie!

Topaz opened a door to a small kitchenette. Tan cabinets lined one side above a counter of white. The floor was tan-and-white-checked linoleum. Not a dolphin in sight. I guessed the ship's designers had saved the mammals for the passengers.

"This is our private sanctuary," she said, opening the well-stocked refrigerator. Sometimes it gets too busy to leave for a meal, so the crew's kitchen keeps it set up for us. Here's the coffeepot. When you drain it, remake. Instructions are on the side, and here's the coffee." She opened a cabinet filled with all kinds of blends and even different tea bags.

I could have used a swig of English Breakfast right then.

Topaz concluded my tour of the "sanctuary" with the far wall of cabinets. "Each one of us has our own, for private-stock snacks." She opened the last door. "Yours would be . . . shit."

Shit? What the heck did that mean? Exactly what kinds of snacks was I in for?

Topaz's cheeks drained of color. I turned to the cabinet, which was filled with stuff—cookies, books, even a file box, which seemed out of place in a kitchenette unless it held recipes.

Messy, yes. But hardly a frightening sight.

Topaz took her hand away from the cabinet door. And merely looked at me.

"That my space?"

"Remy's," she whispered.

Yikes. That "stuff" was Remy's? Talk about a find! "Oh, how sad. Look, Topaz. Fix yourself a coffee, go on back out and leave cleaning the cabinet to me. I'll just toss everything. Okay?"

Please say "okay" and get the heck out of here so I can snoop.

She nodded and left without fixing herself a coffee. Great. I reached up for Remy's bag of Reese's peanut butter cups. My hand froze in midair. It was kinda spooky, touching the stuff of a missing man.

Maybe a dead man.

Jackie's fate had me thinking along those lines more and more lately. I told myself to calm down, that I didn't know Remy personally and so had no emotional sorrow to prevent me from cleaning and snooping. I touched the bag of candy.

No electric shocks. No premonitions of where Remy might be. And no lump in my throat.

The bag landed in the trash along with a box of tea bags, which I could never bring myself to use, and all the other boxes and bags of snacks. Remy had to have worked out a lot to have such a good physique and be able to eat all this junk food.

When I touched the file box, I shut my eyes a second and prayed there would be something useful in it for me. I gave a quick eye sweep of the room. Topaz was gone—back at the front desk, I felt certain. Peter wasn't there, nor was Rico, who I learned at breakfast was going to orient me today.

Betty must have traded shifts after her "date" last night. Way to go, Betty!

I smiled to myself and grabbed the box. Not sure what I'd find, I thought of the old fable of the lady and the tiger. If she picked the wrong door, she'd be eaten. What might happen to me? I held on to the top of the box for a few seconds before moving it. Maybe something would jump out at me! Maybe there'd be some dead mouse, who'd eaten Remy's snacks, in the box.

I leaned against the wall and gingerly opened the top.

"Geez!"

Twelve

I stifled a scream as I watched a tiny black spider hightail it out of the file box. I shook my head and was damn glad Jagger wasn't around to tease me unabashedly.

After I chastised myself and decided most women (and lots of men) hated spiders or any crawly things, I looked into the box. A Swiss army knife, very worn, a broken compass, a few old receipts for purchases of clothing and cologne from duty-free shops in Bermuda and a key.

Hmm. A key. Pay dirt?

I should have turned the box over to the captain, but gave myself permission, with the logic that I needed it for my case, to keep the key for twenty-four hours.

Despite the fact that I had no idea what it was to, I stuck it in my pocket and shut the box. Then I took a few paper towels and some Windex to wipe out the inside of what was now my cabinet. Not that I had anything to put into it, but I thought it was better cleansed of any Remy reminders.

Or spider food.

After I threw out the paper towels, I took the box and headed toward the reception desk. Rico and Topaz were playing cards.

"Slow morning?"

They looked at me.

"Oh, hey, *amore*, how are you doing?" Rico asked. He looked at the box. "Taking notes about all of us?" He laughed.

My eyes widened. Did he suspect something? I forced a laugh to hide any guilty look that might come across my face and set the box down. "Ha. Ha. Good one." I leaned closer to him. "You've exposed me. I am an international spy. Got something to hide?" I laughed then said, "Seriously, I found this in my kitchenette cabinet."

"Remy's old cabinet," Topaz clarified.

They looked at each other. I couldn't see Rico's face, but thought Topaz looked as if she knew something that I didn't. Geez. Was this the ship of ghouls or ship of fools? And was I the number-one fool?

It seemed as if they all had some secret, or at least things they weren't sharing with me. There was something going on behind the scenes and no one was letting me see the dress rehearsal.

"What should I do with this?" I set it down on the counter. They glared at it and then looked up at me. "My personal take is that I think it should go to the captain."

Rico nodded. "Sounds like a plan. What's inside anyway?"

I touched the top then stopped. "I have no idea. I didn't open it. Didn't feel right to pry."

"I'll pry away," Topaz said, yanking the top open. "Shit. Him and that stupid knife. Carried it with him. Used to practice throwing it at the walls on the lower deck. If the captain knew. Shit. Odd that old Remy didn't take it with him."

Odd indeed.

Maybe that's why he'd used a steak knife to kill Jackie.

Rico laughed while I wondered if they bought the fact that I said I hadn't looked inside. I peeked behind Rico to the golden-mirrored wall to see if I looked guilty.

Naw.

Maybe I really was developing in my new profession. After three cases, I proclaimed that I was. I was nearly a full time fraud investigator, working my first case *alone*.

Just because Jagger was on the ship as reinforcement, didn't mean I had to share everything with him.

And look how far I'd gotten!

* * *

"And a key," I told Jagger, after deciding I was smart enough to know when to use the skills of my reinforcement and mentor. On my lunch break, I'd caught him playing shuffleboard with the young kitten who never seemed to like my interfering and was always around "Jay."

Jagger introduced her as Bobbie Lee from Alabama. Southern debutante, I "declared" to myself and then felt a strong urge to slap the "darling" for being so domineering of my Jagger. Of Jagger that is. Of course he wasn't *mine*.

Bobbie Lee indeed. What kind of name was that for a girl anyway? A young, sexy and Southern girl. Ha. No wonder the possessiveness with her Jay. I think she would have shoved me overboard if given half the chance.

I held onto the railing, so glad to see the seas calm and the sun sparkling on the crests of the waves. And Jagger in shorts.

Bermuda white shorts. Part of the hot-weather uniform.

Damn, but he had dynamite legs!

A storm of heat spun inside me now. What a day this was turning out to be.

After I tore my vision from Jagger's legs—and yes, he did notice me staring and shook his head at me, I let go of the railing (but never turned my back on Bobbie Dear) and touched Jagger's arm. "Could I have a moment with you? Please."

He gave me an odd look, and then said to his

"date," "Excuse me for a few minutes. Why don't you go get us each a lemonade? Put them on my tab, of course."

At first I thought she'd break out in tears and have a temper tantrum, much like my two-year-old nephew was known to do, right in the middle of the shuffleboard court. But she rolled her eyes at me, gave Jagger a saucy smile and turned toward the bar. I don't think kitten Bobbie ever served anyone lemonade in her life.

I bit my tongue before saying, "I thought she'd never leave, and what the heck are you doing with her? I think there are statutory rape laws even out at sea." I yanked Jagger toward the dolphin tank and found a quiet spot away from the bar. Nice and secluded.

"What's going on?" he asked, sitting in the shade.

The guy didn't even burn in the sun. Only turned a healthy golden shade. Then I clarified what I had started to tell him about the case, the box and my cabinet, and said, "We really need to find out more about Remy. I think he's the solution to all of this."

Jagger ran his hand through his hair.

I looked away. Gilbert the dolphin looked at me, and I think he smiled. Or maybe grinned. Men.

Several passengers surrounding the pool looked at me. After a gracious smile, I turned back.

"You're right, Sherlock."

Damn, that felt good. "But how?"

He looked at me. I thought he was going to say that it was my problem, but instead he said, "Let me get Bobbie Lee settled, and I'll meet you in the infirmary."

Get rid of Bobbie Lee, was more like it, I thought.

I felt something on my arm and swung around. Bobbie Lee stood there glaring. Oh . . . my . . . God! Had I said that out loud?

Jagger didn't seem to notice, so I went with the assumption she didn't hear me, but she must have gotten some well-deserved bad vibes from me anyway.

"You promised to spend the morning with me, Jay. I'm afraid I'm not too pleased with all . . . of this." She took her hand away from my shoulder and swept it through the air to indicate "this" included me.

Not too pleased with me, kiddo? Ha. You ain't seen nothing yet. I got up and turned toward her . . . then stopped. I couldn't say a thing without giving away the fact that Jagger and I were working together. But boy, did I want to let her have it.

"Well, I'll leave you two alone. I have to get back to work anyway."

Jagger sat there silently. I know he had to be fuming inside. One thing I knew Jagger would not like was two females fawning all over him. Bobbie Lee was treading on thin ice. Me, I kept my fantasies in my head where they belonged.

"Oh, Hunter!" Bobbie Lee called out.

Before I turned to look were she was waving, I hoped there was someone else on the ship named Hunter.

"Ah, what have we here?" Hunter Knight asked.

Damn. I swung around. "Oh, hey. How's it going?"

"I'm fine, Pauline. Nice seeing you. How is work?"

Maybe he was trying to tell me to get back to my job, but I took a quick look at my watch to see I had fifteen minutes left. I could stay here and see what went down between Jagger and Hunter.

Hunter gave Jagger a very unpleasant look. "Are you on a break?"

Oh, boy. I'd nearly forgotten that Hunter was Jagger's boss. By the way Jagger sat there staring, I guess he hadn't forgotten but sure would like to.

"I'm working, Knight. Bobbie Lee and I are taking a break from shuffleboard for a lemonade."

Hunter looked at the table and at both of their hands. No drinks in sight.

"Oh, I forgot to get the lemonades," Bobbie Lee said and then laughed. "Got busy talking to Mike the bartender."

Now *I* shook my head.

After a bit of small talk, I said, "Well, I do have to get going."

Bobbie Lee never did go get their drinks. I think she didn't want to leave Jagger's side. As if I would snatch him away. She looked really upset with both of us as I nodded and walked past the tank, giving a smile to Gilbert and his friends.

When I got to the elevator, I looked back and saw Hunter talking to Jagger with no Bobbie Lee around—Hunter not looking all too pleased.

And Jagger looking very pissed.

I had to smile to myself as I got on the elevator. I'm sure Jagger wanted to deck Hunter and probably throw the Southern belle overboard. How tempting was that on a ship?

With only one wrong turn, I made it back to the infirmary with five minutes to spare.

The rest of the afternoon went calmly with only a few cases of seasickness, two cuts that needed butterfly bandages and one of the swinging singles who'd had way too much sun and rum.

Rico did a good job of showing me around, and I started to feel very comfortable in the job. Hopefully, there'd be no big emergencies. I really wanted everyone onboard to stay safe and have a good time. I was wondering what my friends and family were doing when the door opened and Uncle Walt came in holding his cheek.

I jumped up and ran to him. "What happened? Come sit down."

I started to show him into the exam room, but Topaz jumped up. "No medical care until I get all his insurance information!" She nearly screamed, as if I was committing some crime.

"He's my uncle. I'll give you the info as soon as we find out what happened."

Uncle Walt took his hand from his cheek, exposing a red mark—in the shape of a hand.

"Oh, my gosh! Someone hit you?" I popped a cold pack with my hands so the chemicals inside would react, and it instantly turned cold. I gently touched it against his cheek. "You may have a shiner tomorrow. Who did this?"

Uncle Walt sheepishly looked at me, then at Rico and at Peter, who had come in the room too. "Seems as if an unhappy passenger didn't think I was doing my job correctly. She wanted me to spend the entire day with her. Um, alone. I'm not like *that*, Pauline. You know it."

I think my face turned redder than Uncle Walt's. Before I could ask who she was, the door to the reception area swung open and a woman in her seventies, I guessed, swept in. Her white suit with navy trim looked expensive but went well with the aura of wealth she exuded.

"*How* is Walter, ya'll? Is he all right?"

I gasped.

Bobbie Lee with a few wrinkles and sags.

But still a looker.

Uncle Walt pulled back as if afraid she'd slug him again, and said, "That is her. Anna Bell Lee."

"Bobbie's mother," I mumbled.

"I know it's hard to believe, but Bobbie's *grand-mother*," Anna Bell corrected as she stepped forward until Topaz blocked her way.

"You can't go in there," she said.

I was ready to deck the woman myself. What was with the Lee women? I guessed they were very used to getting their own way with their men.

Poor Uncle Walt looked as if he wanted to crawl under the stretcher to escape.

The doc said he needed to finish examining Uncle Walt's injury and make sure his vision wasn't impaired.

A remorseful Anna Bell sat herself in the waiting room and kept repeating that she really didn't mean anything, but she just wanted Uncle Walt to . . . keep her company. "The passenger always comes first," she said.

Since Rico was helping the doc, I walked over to Anna Bell, quite fed up with the Lee clan. "Look, my uncle is the perfect gentleman. Maybe you are used to having whatever you want, but he's not up for grabs." I smiled to myself at the pun. "So, I would appreciate if you would leave him alone. Find someone else to keep you busy, or I'll have the captain notified of your attack on Uncle Walt—and your trip will terminate in Miami."

I wanted to add that her granddaughter would be thrown off along with her, but figured Jagger could handle her.

Anna Bell merely looked at me. In the reflection of the mirror, I noticed Topaz grin and realized I'd gained another brownie point with her.

"Well, as long as he is all right. I only came down here to make sure." She got up and turned toward the door.

Yeah, right, I thought. "I'm glad we have all of this settled. Enjoy the rest of your cruise, ma'am," I added. I wanted to give her a swift kick in the butt. However, even I wouldn't kick an old lady.

Uncle Walt was proclaimed in perfect health, should expect a black eye and to watch out for any headaches or nausea. I leaned over and whispered to him, "And stick with Yankee women. You're out of your league in the South."

He smiled and left after Topaz finished the insurance information. I looked over her shoulder and had to bite my tongue before I yelled that the fee for the visit was outrageous.

"Isn't he considered staff?" I asked.

"Nope. Male hosts don't get paid. They only get a free ride." With that she turned to the printer and pushed a button to finish her billing process.

I leaned against the wall and thought that I really needed to find out who got all that money. I could see my family doctor ten times for that price. "Topaz, do you ever have trouble getting the insurance companies to pay the claims?" I figured I'd take a shot since she'd become my new best friend.

She took the paper from the printer and looked at me. "Nope. Not that I know of. Some folks in a land office in New York handle the final billing. How could the insurance companies argue anyway? Where else can the passengers go for care when we're out in the middle of the ocean?"

I nodded. "Oh, right." But who gets all the money? And who works in that land office?

While I stood there stunned, the door opened and Jagger walked in wearing his black jeans, a black tee and his sunglasses on his head.

As delicious as he looked in the Bermuda shorts, *this* was my Jagger.

He motioned for me to come to the side of the room.

Topaz gave him the once-over and said, "I have to go fax this." After one more look at Jagger, she left.

"Some old lady hit Uncle Walt because he wouldn't . . . er . . . spend time with her."

Jagger's eyes darkened. "Is he all right?"

I smiled at his concern for my uncle. Jagger had a special spot in his heart for the old man and even let him drive his SUV on occasion—when at his age, Uncle Walt shouldn't have been driving at all.

"Some of these passengers are . . . whackos," he said.

"Yeah. Oh, I'm off duty now so we can start working the case. We'll be docking in Miami pretty soon, so lots of the passengers will get off for a few hours. We might have better luck snooping together—"

"I'm afraid you're on your own, Sherlock."

Thirteen

I'm afraid you're on your own, Sherlock?

I waited a few seconds to process the meaning of what Jagger had said. No clue. What the hell did he mean? "What are you talking about? On my *own*?"

"Darling Bobbie got me fired. Made your buddy Hunter's day, I'm sure. I'm off the ship in Miami, lock, stock and barrel."

"Whaaat?" I meant to say that Hunter was not my buddy, but couldn't get it out. Couldn't get anything coherent out. Jagger was leaving? "Whaaat?" I repeated.

He touched my chin, lifting my jaw shut. "Hunter fired me after Bobbie Lee gave him a piece of her mind."

"So she has nothing left, then."

We looked at each other and laughed—although I really wasn't in a laughing mood after that bomb he'd just dropped on me. "They can't do this to you. You're a passenger, for crying out loud." Then I thought of my threat to Anna Bell.

"It's a private cruise line, Sherlock. They make their own rules for certain things. They can and did do what the hell they want. After all, I'm not a paying passenger."

I bit my lower lip before it had a chance to quiver.

Jagger took me by the shoulders. "You can do this on your own, Sherlock. You *can*."

For a second, I actually believed him. I puffed out my chest and stood taller. "Yeah, I can," I said, and then realized it was a lie.

Even knowing Goldie and Miles were onboard for emergencies, I wanted Jagger around too. Some girls had their comfort food, like mashed potatoes and gravy or chocolate or wine, but me, I had . . . my Jagger.

He took me into his arms and held me for a long time. When he let go, he leaned forward and kissed me. On the lips.

And I was so damned glad I'd let him.

And for one magical moment, I believed everything *would be* all right.

"Oh my God. Oh my God!" Goldie shouted when I told him and Miles about Jagger getting kicked off the ship.

They wrapped me in a group hug, reminding

me that they would be there for me. Much more available than they had been. I looked at their lean, sun-tanned bodies and said, "I can't ask you guys to give up your vacation. Not even a little bit of it. I'm going to be all right on my own."

They glared at me.

Goldie bit down on his pinky fingernail, today a royal, ocean blue.

"Jagger said so."

They paused then nodded. "Go for it, Suga."

I winked and told them I wanted to see Jagger one more time before he left the ship to fly back to Hope Valley. I would have thought an emptiness should settle in my insides now, but I actually felt pretty good. I touched the necklace of pepper spray Jagger had given me and symbolically told myself it would give me strength and the knowledge to finish this case . . . alone.

My friends offered to go watch the passengers leave the ship and see if we could find Jagger, but I said I'd be fine on my own.

Soon I stood on the upper deck, watching all the activity below. Passengers disembarking. Cabs honking to get fares, and loading and unloading of supplies from the side of the ship.

Several security people were obviously keeping very close tabs on who left the ship. The dock bustled with so much activity that my head hurt flipping it back and forth to search the crowds for Jagger.

When the last of the passengers left, I started to turn, disappointed that I'd missed him. Then I noticed two security officers walking down the plank with a man in between. Even from this distance I could tell it was my buddy.

My Jagger.

No one else had that good a physique from the back. A cab sat waiting at the curb, and I became angry that they were treating him like some kind of criminal. I pictured the Lee women falling overboard and made a mental note not to get too close to Bobbie when on the decks for fear that my fantasy would come true—at the touch of my fingertips.

"Bye," I whispered.

As if he could hear, Jagger turned around, zoomed in on me, gave me a salute of encouragement and mouthed, "You can do it, Sherlock."

After a shaky wave to him, I watched the cab drive off with my sometimes partner inside. It wouldn't surprise me if I got an email in a day or so, checking up on me.

What a guy.

I treated myself to a Coors Light after watching Jagger leave. Most of the passengers had disembarked at the Miami port for several hours. When I looked around the Bottlenose Lounge, an eerie feeling took over.

Other than myself and Edie, who was busy re-stocking the supplies along with several other crewmembers, there was only one man, reading a book, sitting in the lounge near the tank.

Johnny, Jake and Gilbert swam lazily around in circles. Even they must have sensed the quiet of the ship. I looked at the bar staff and decided they weren't going to be of any help. I had to get back to work. So I finished my Coors and left a tip for Edie, then walked toward the tank. Without touching the glass, I put my hand up as if to wave.

Gilbert swam over, his eyes saddened while he nuzzled the glass. I had to smiled. "Atta boy."

Atta girl, Sherlock.

Damn. Jagger always said that to me when I did something right during a case. I shook the cobwebs of nostalgia out of my head, actually did wave to Gilbert and turned to leave.

"Interesting creatures," the man sitting near the tank said as he set his book down on the table.

"Oh. Yes, they are." I really wasn't in the mood to give him my zoology lesson about the buffeo dolphins. Besides, by the looks of him, he probably already knew more about them than I did.

Looking very much the professor, with wire-rimmed glasses, a houndstooth jacket with suede patches on the elbows and a peppered gray-and-brown beard to match his shoulder-length hair, he came across as being quite the scholar.

I froze on the spot. Jagger! He'd been known to disguise himself and show up at the opportune time. I leaned near and said, "You dog, you. And here I thought you were gone!"

The man looked at me as if *I* were "gone."

"Pardon me, ma'am?" He eased back a bit.

I pulled the chair next to him with my foot and flopped down. "How the heck did you manage that? Getting back and changed so fast? You are a Houdini, for sure."

I went to slap him on the back, but he pulled away. "What? Well, I never. You'll have to leave or I'll call someone."

I winked at him.

I leaned even closer to whisper but bit my tongue when I noticed the pale blue eyes, which certainly were not contacts. Oops. I realized my error. How to get away without being reported to security?

"Henry, right?"

He hesitated. "No. Jonathan. Jonathan Wentworth."

"Oh my." I laughed and flew up from my seat. "I'm so sorry. I'm mistaken. You look very much like Henry . . . Tan . . . Tanker from New Jersey."

Gilbert swam by that second to help me with my lie. The man smiled and seemed to buy it. With that I apologized again and hurried out before he changed his mind.

* * *

My first thought was to go back to the infirmary and look around, but figured the staff would think I was too strange, coming back on my time off, since I'd already made it through my first shift without incident. So I went to my cabin to change out of my uniform. Once I was more comfortable, I'd get back to work.

Even if I had no clue as to where to go to do it.

Betty was sitting in the chair by the porthole doing a seascape needlepoint. She told me that another nurse, who had sailed with her before, joined the crew in Miami.

"Oh. Is she taking Jackie's place?"

Betty looked up. "Yes. She's a seasoned cruise-ship nurse, so no need for orientation. Kristina Archambault. She just worked her last cruise on this ship a month ago. Great luck."

I nodded. "Yeah. It's still so sad about Jackie."

Betty stuck the needle through the material with more force than necessary. I wondered if she really missed the woman whom she seemed to dislike or maybe was more frightened that the killer hadn't been caught yet.

The investigation continued behind the scenes so the passengers and crewmembers weren't privy to much of what was going on. Obviously my parents hadn't even heard about the murder—or I'm sure they would have been on the flight home with Jagger.

I took some jeans and a lightweight top from

my drawer then turned to see Betty still working on her needlepoint. After working a cruise for a long time, I would think it could get kinda boring when off duty. "Don't you leave the ship on your time off, Betty?"

"Not much to see or do in Miami when you've been here oodles of times." She chuckled.

"I hadn't thought about that. So, what do you like to do?"

"You sure ask a lot of questions."

Yikes. I couldn't tell by her tone if that was a casual remark or not.

Without taking her head from her work, she asked, "How come *you* haven't gone ashore?"

Good question. "Oh. Well, I really don't like the heat and humidity that much," I lied, when I really had been eager to step on dry land to at least say I'd been to Miami. But I had work to do and now that a new, experienced nurse was here—and she might shed some light on my case—there was no way I could leave the ship.

Betty seemed to buy my excuse and kept to herself even after I came out of the bathroom all changed. I said I'd see her later and went out the door. I looked both ways and wished I'd asked her what cabin Kristina was in so I could pay a "welcome wagon" call.

Someone on duty might know, so I went to the infirmary. Topaz and Rico were off duty since they worked the shift with me. Peter was sitting at the desk with a dark-haired woman who looked about my age. She looked up and said, "May I help you?"

Before I could speak, Peter was up and introducing us. "Pauline is a new nurse onboard. Filling in for... Remy. Pauline, this is Kris Archambault."

Kristina, I thought. Great. I did the usual cordial welcome and sat on the edge of the desk while Peter got up to get us all coffee. If I drank coffee at this time of the night, I'd be awake until dawn, when my next shift started, but at least sending him for drinks got rid of him. I thought it strange that a doctor would offer to get nurses coffee, but I wasn't going to argue. He always appeared to be a gentleman.

"I understand you've worked on the *Golden Dolphin* before?" I asked Kris. Not much taller than myself, Kris looked about my age.

She nodded and seemed very pleasant and, despite her last name, which was French Canadian—and her ex-husband's, she told me—she spoke with a slight German accent.

I wasn't sure if she knew whom she was replacing, but decided the only way to find out was to ask. "Did you know Jackie?"

"Jackie. I'm so terribly upset about that. When personnel called me to fill in for the rest of this cruise, I was shocked to hear about her."

Not as shocked as I was to *find* her.

"Did you know her very well?" *Please. Please give me something to go on here.*

Unlike the very proper Betty, Kristina was very open. She reminded me of the free spirits of the sixties (the ones I'd seen in movies, since I was way too young to have experienced it. I don't think she even wore a bra although if she did, it would be an A cup).

I looked toward the kitchenette to see if Peter was on his way back. No sign of him. Good. Maybe he had to make a new pot of coffee or face the wrath of Topaz.

Kris turned toward the computer and clicked on PRINT. Soon the printer whizzed and coughed out a few sheets.

I reached into my pocket and took out Remy's key. "I was hoping Rico would be around."

"Aren't we all? What a piece he is." She chuckled a low rather sexy sound.

Hmm. Was there something going on between them? Sometimes I felt as if I were sailing through a soap opera. Maybe there was something about the Bermuda Triangle after all. Or, in reality, maybe it was because these folks were cooped up on a cruise ship, often stuck out at sea for weeks on end, and turned to each other for fun and comfort.

And sometimes fraud.

"Yes—" I laughed. "Rico is a doll. Actually there are several dolls onboard." The key felt hot in my hand as if reminding me to find out what I could. "I know you weren't on the ship at the beginning of this cruise, but does this look familiar to you? Do you know what it is?" I opened my palm.

"It's a key." She got up, took the papers from the printer. Then she turned to me, standing there with my stupid hand spread out. "Sorry. I couldn't resist." She looked closer. "It looks to me like one of the keys for the janitor's closets or the stock rooms down below. Where the engines are and the mechanics work. All the state rooms have card keys."

While I processed all the possibilities, she looked at me. "Where'd you get it? Maybe that would help."

Yikes. Now I had to bring out my Oscar-winning lie. "Oh. I found it." Meryl Streep I was not today.

"There's a lost and found. Give it to Adam Watt, the ship's purser. Have you met him?" She shoved some papers into the out-box.

"No." And I don't intend to just yet. "Well, I'll let you get back to work. Tell Peter thanks for the coffee, but I don't do caffeine so late." There were no patients waiting, but I had to say something to get out of there and go start checking doors.

"Yeah, I'll rush right over to take care of all these passengers!" She laughed.

I like Kris, I thought as I walked out, clutching my pepper-spray locket.

I just might need that locket as I tried to find out what this key unlocked.

I made a quick trip to my cabin to get my miniature camera disguised as a beeper and attached it to the waistband of my jeans. Betty wasn't there, which I was glad to see, so I wouldn't have to explain what the heck I was doing with a beeper, and me not even on call. I yanked my shirt out of my pants so that it covered the camera. One final check in the mirror to make sure I looked innocent, and I was out the door and down the hallway.

I knew the general direction of the other crew's quarters, but still had no idea how to get to the lower part of the ship. I planned to take the next set of downward stairs that I found.

The ship was to stay in the Miami harbor until morning, so I had plenty of time to investigate. When I opened a fire door between two hallways, I heard lots of noise. For a second I hesitated and almost turned back, but instead, I stayed and listened.

Laughter.

Shouting.

Music.

Didn't sound too ominous. I slipped into the second hallway and turned a corner. It looked as if the entire crew was settled along the floor, standing in the middle or walking through the hallway.

Rico turned around and shouted, "Hey, *amore*! Come join the hallway party!"

Before I could say a thing, Rico grabbed me and was introducing me to all the staff, mostly guys. Seemed they often got together in the hallway to have a few beers and party out of the view of the captain and passengers. No one was rowdy, and they all seemed very nice.

Someone handed me a Coors in a bottle, and Rico chastised them for not giving "a lady" a plastic cup. "I prefer mine from the bottle," I yelled to the cheers of the guys around me.

When I took my first sip, I thought I should be investigating, but then realized, after looking over this crowd, that half of these guys probably worked down below.

Where the key might fit.

I started to work the crowd, getting to know some really nice guys. One of them, Eduardo Castillo, who said to call him "Eddie," and told me he was the motorman. He was sitting on the floor at the far end of the hallway.

I laughed and sat next to him when he gestured toward the floor. "Is that anything like Superman?"

With a grin, he said, "*Sí*, I am like the Superman—" He leaned forward and leered at me, but I knew he was teasing. As I laughed, he said, "But really my job is to take care and clean parts of the engines."

Bingo.

"Well, Superman Eddie, that sounds interesting. I can't imagine how huge the engines must be to run a ship like this." I chuckled and took a swig of my beer. "The biggest engine I ever saw was under the hood of my Volvo."

We both laughed.

Eddie got up and reached out his hand to me. "Come, Paulina, I will show you a big engine."

"That's not like 'come to my place and I'll show you my etchings' is it?" I grabbed his hand and stood up.

Eddie laughed. "I am married. My wife and children, three of them, live back in Ecuador. I send them money and go home when I can."

Phew. At least I didn't have to play up to Eddie to get to see the downstairs. "That's great. Lead the way, Motorman."

We said goodbye to the rest of the crew and Eddie told Rico what our plans were.

"Sounds like the highlight of your trip, *amore*."

Better than a murder in my cabin, I thought, but said, "I'm really excited to see the workings of this thing!"

In true gentlemanly fashion, Eddie gave me the grand tour, introducing me to all the crewmembers as we met them. Several were engineers who worked the gigantic computerized ivory panel opposite a wall of pale green with switches, knobs and red lights running the entire length.

The room was very narrow, but I guessed that made it easier to see the panel from the other side.

Eddie seemed animated when he gave me the tour—and, although I kept looking for locks that the key might fit, I was actually enjoying myself. It was amazing what it took to power this ship. I'd love to be down there when the ship actually set sail in the morning.

Hopefully I would have some information before tomorrow.

"And this is where I work," Eddie said proudly.

"Neat." I looked around the sparkling-clean room. There was a chugging sound and an oily smell. The area had several levels, with iron grid walkways leading to parts of what Eddie called the "heart of the ship."

"Looks as if you keep the place spotless."

He beamed with pride. "*Gracias*, Paulina."

I looked at my watch and realized it was getting late. Not a night person, I would be hard-pressed to get up tomorrow if I didn't get my eight hours of beauty rest. I yawned.

"Oh, boy. Someone is tired."

"Yeah. I think I'll head back."

"I'll walk you to the infirmary area. It is not too easy to find your way around here sometimes."

Thankful, I smiled, but in reality planned to ditch Eddie to snoop around. What better excuse than to say I got "lost" if someone found me?

Just then, a crewmember in a royal blue jump-suit came up the steps. "Oh, Eduardo. Perfect timing. David needs to find the tools that he claims were left near the number-two generator. Have you seen them, man?" The guy nodded politely at me when he finished speaking to Eddie.

There is a God.

Eddie made a quick introduction and let me convince him that I could find my way "home." Soon I was outside the engine room with the key pressed into my hand—inside my pocket.

Kris had been correct. There were plenty of doors around here that had key locks instead of card keys. I took out the key, said a fast prayer and started to turn door handles. If they didn't open, I stuck the key in and tried to turn. After an hour, I really *was* lost and had seen enough closets and supply rooms to last a lifetime.

It seemed as if I'd passed the engine room three times, but no one was around to give me directions—and believe me, I wasn't above asking. I thought of Jagger and smiled to myself. He'd never admit to being lost or ask how to find his way.

Suddenly I missed him. Not for help with my case—since I was proud I'd gotten this far—but more . . . as a friend. Working crime was a lot of common sense, which was something I had.

I walked to the end of the hallway and stopped. Which way to take? Down the right corridor several guys were working on changing light bulbs in the ceiling fixtures. The left corridor was empty.

I took the left.

All the doors were numbered and labeled, which I thought was for fire purposes. Someone would need to know that information to find the area on such a large vessel. With the key still in my hand, I turned knobs as I went along.

Three were locked doors but my key didn't fit. At the end of the hallway was the emergency exit and a door leading to a set of stairs. But underneath the stairs was an unmarked door. Paint peeled a bit on the wall near the door. Seemed odd on a ship that was kept so top notch.

Actually, the peeling looked like a little dolphin. How appropriate. I could use it as my marker for where to resume my search for what door the key fit.

After three more yawns, I gave up tonight's search. I mimicked Scarlet O'Hara in my head with *"Tomorrow is another day,"* and then started up the stairs.

I heard footsteps coming down toward me.

Shoot. I really didn't feel like taking the time to explain what the heck I was doing here. So I turned and flew down the stairs and toward the unmarked room. I grabbed the handle and turned. Nothing. Damn!

Now two people were talking. Male voices. I

stuck the key in the lock, said, "Come on, Saint Theresa, give me a break here," and turned.

The lock clicked.

The door opened.

I stepped into the darkness and hid there, holding the door open just enough to see the two crewmembers walk past. Phew again. When they left, I opened the door, allowing the bright light of the corridor to highlight the room.

"Oh . . . my . . . God."

Fourteen

Stella Sokol always used to tell us kids that prayers were not always answered and there is a good reason why. However, she was never able to give us any reason other than "because they are or they are not."

Sensing that I was alone, I flipped on the light switch and looked at the room I'd taken refuge in.

Saint Theresa had come through like gangbusters.

I said a quick thanks and walked into the tiny space to observe a bed, which looked as if it'd been squeezed into the tiny place, and an olive drab duffel bag lying on the floor with clothing spewing out. What originally caught my attention was the pair of white sneakers, a pair of white slacks and a white shirt with the epaulets on the shoulders—exactly like mine.

Exactly like Rico's, Betty's and Kristina's.

A crew nursing uniform.

A man's.

Remy Girard's.

I leaned closer to a box that was turned upside down for a makeshift table. Framed in brass and silver was the photo of Jackie, Betty and Remy— all smiling—and him wearing a salmon-colored tee shirt that said BERMUDA on the front in bold yellow.

Remy Girard was indeed alive and living on this ship!

My hand flew to my mouth to stifle a gasp although I felt sure no one was around to hear me. After my hand stopped shaking, I decided I needed to report my find to the safety officer and in turn the FBI. But first I took a few shots with my beeper camera. Remy easily could have killed Jackie and no one would have known, since he was missing and thought dead. He must have kept the extra key in the kitchenette in case he lost one or had to jump ship and come back in disguise.

How clever the guy must be.

Clever enough to be running an insurance-fraud scam from the bowels of the *Golden Dolphin*—and nearly getting away with *murder*.

It only took me forty-eight minutes to find my way back to the main body of the ship and to ask where the safety officer's office was. A few times I had to duck into the nearest open door when I thought I heard someone behind me. No one could be following me, because, after all, how could they know who I was? Before I knew it, I was telling William Benoit, the safety officer; the captain and the FBI suits about my find. I told them who I really was and turned over the key to the blond one.

I was ready to defend myself in case they thought I was a nutcase, but Captain Duarte said they had known who I was from the beginning. I was floored, but realized Jagger must have something to do with that (and well, this *was* the FBI). I imagined they even knew about all the parking tickets I'd gotten throughout the years.

Obviously Jagger had told them to protect me, or right now I think I'd be sitting in some uncomfortable straight chair beneath a naked lightbulb in a dark room, facing interrogation by Miami's finest and the FBI crew.

Hmm. If Jagger had shared his cover with them, how come he'd gotten thrown off the ship? Was that a cover too? Was I going to "run into" him in some darkened hallway one of these nights?

One never knew, where Jagger was concerned.

A sense of relief washed over me, especially since I had found and taken pictures of several checks in Remy's room with the invoices showing that two thirds of the payments went to insurance carriers and one third to our fraud criminals. They had been made out to "cash." Once the photos were developed, I'd find his accomplices and be going home soon.

"But whom is he still working with?" the captain asked. "Who knows that Mr. Gerard is on this ship and is in cahoots with him?"

"Good question. Seems as if we think alike," I said. "That was my next plan. To find out the answer to that."

The suit with the blond hair said, "We'll make a thorough check, ma'am."

Ma'am? The way he said it made me sound so old. I didn't want to argue with a Fed, so I just smiled silently, thinking, *I'm not giving up on my case, buddy. Not while Fabio holds the key to my paycheck.*

Captain Duarte stood. "Please show us this hideaway, Ms. Sokol."

Whoa, boy. I didn't think they'd be real pleased with me for taking forty-eight minutes to show them the way. I smiled and said, "Follow me," all the while praying I could trace my steps backward faster than I found it the first time.

When we passed the gift shop twice, I decided I wasn't above the truth—in order to not anger the FBI guy, who, by the way, was not really pleased to see the gift shop again.

"Well, unless the ship has two identical gift shops, I seem to have lost my bearings. Maybe the

Bermuda Triangle has something to do with it." I said and then laughed.

The captain gave me a fatherly smile.

Mr. Benoit stood silent and glaring.

And the blond FBI guy said, "Perhaps, ma'am, if you tell the captain what the area looked like, he can get us there . . . faster."

As if I couldn't. Well! I gave Captain Duarte a good description (Leaving out the chipped paint dolphin on the wall. I didn't want them to think I was crazy, like some people who see the Virgin Mary on walls or made out of potato chips.). He frowned (I'm sure wondering what the heck I was doing down there in the first place, since my case was in the medical area), and then we were on our way—miles away from where the gift shop was.

"There. There it is!" I said, nearly shouting after we'd turned a corner in the hallway. I looked at my watch. Thirty-seven minutes, including the double trip by the gift shop. *Not bad*, I thought, until I looked at the annoyed yet good-looking, face of the FBI guy.

"That room has been used for storage. There should have been boxes in it," Captain Duarte said.

I eased past the safety office and the FBI guy. "Well, one box was still left. Mr. Girard had it turned upside down like a table. He had a picture of himself, Jackie and Betty on it."

Mr. Benoit took out what must have been a master key and stuck it in the lock. When it clicked and he reached for the door handle, I said, "I guess Remy is the number-one suspect in Jackie's murder?"

The door opened in a second, Mr. Benoit flipped on the light and I heard the blond guy mutter, "Christ."

The room was completely empty.

With Captain Duarte in the lead, we made our way back to his office in less than ten minutes. He opened his door and waved a hand for us all to pass.

I wanted to turn and run. I'd been apologizing and mumbling how the stuff really was in the room when I saw it.

The blond Fed didn't believe me. I could tell.

But Captain Duarte said, "I'm sure it was, Ms. Sokol." Although I think he was lying.

And Mr. Benoit, obviously feeling sorry for me, said, "Criminals like to cover their tracks."

"Which means Remy is still onboard!" *And knows that I found his hiding place.* Now my life was in danger.

The other FBI agent asked me if anyone had seen me earlier, when I'd been looking for this supposed room. I told him about the footsteps behind me and how I had to duck into the room after I opened it with the key.

They chatted for a while and concluded that I should be more careful. The blond suggested to the captain that I not be allowed to investigate anywhere but around the infirmary. I heard him say something about a bodyguard, but the guy was a master at hiding what he didn't want others to hear. "For her own safety," he'd said.

Holding back the urge to slug him, I said, "I can take care of myself, *sir*." *There. Take that.* He looked about my age, but my calling him "sir" made me feel younger.

"Everyone says that." He turned toward the captain, who stood there with a pitiable look on his face—for me.

"I'm sure Agent Harwinton (the blond) only has your safety in mind. It might be a good idea to stay away from secluded areas until Mr. Girard is in custody.

"Might be a good idea" was *not* the same as being ordered not to go there. Splitting hairs, sure. But still, it kept me from openly disobeying the nice captain.

I bit my tongue from any further discussion so the captain would not clarify his statement.

Before I could open the door, I heard mumbling from the security officer and the blond. I'd bet the guy was talking about me. He was probably going to continue to interfere in my case. So I "accidentally" dropped my lipstick and with help from my toe, it rolled closer to them.

"Damn. The guy's got to be onboard somewhere. First the body shit, now this," Harwinton said.

I paused and ran my hand along the carpet as if looking for my lipstick, which was clearly right in front of his shoe.

I had to find out about the body.

The security officer said, "If Girard is onboard, we'll find him."

"Yeah, but who the hell got to the body while it was secured by your people? It's probably goddamn shark food right now."

I jumped up and covered my mouth with my hand.

Jackie's body was *missing*!

After I'd pulled out of my stupor, managed a few polite goodbyes and gotten my lipstick, I was now safely back in my room snuggled in bed while Betty snored away—and so wound up I knew I'd never sleep tonight.

I only wished I could share my find about Remy's room and subsequent loss of it with Jagger.

That thought kept me more awake than before. Soon I noticed the sun peeking through the porthole and felt the slight motion of the ship. I pressed on my anti-nausea bracelet, which had been working splendidly, and realized we were headed off to Bermuda.

And poor Jackie's body had probably been thrown overboard.

* * *

The next day passed without incident in both my nursing job and in my investigation. I had "wandered" down to Remy's hideout only to find it padlocked and sealed off with yellow tape. I blamed it on the FBI.

Maybe I could have found something more in the room that would help my case, since I had to wait to get my pictures developed in Bermuda— like another picture or note or something that might have been left behind by Remy. I couldn't take a chance on having my pictures developed on board.

Every time I thought of Jackie, my body shivered.

Personally, I would have left the place untouched to use as bait to catch Remy, who might be dumb enough to move back there, even though the room was at the end of a hallway, with no way to set up a stakeout. Guess they had their reasons for doing whatever they did, or maybe they'd found him already. I was assuming the blond wouldn't have shared that info with me.

Damn G-men.

By evening I was off duty and had changed into comfortable ivory slacks and a matching sleeveless top with a pastel rose painted on the front. I stuck my hair up, which always made me look older and more sophisticated or, actually, as if I were going back to work as a nurse. To change that image, I doused myself with my Estee Lauder Beautiful perfume. Feeling kind of lonely now that Jagger was gone, I decided I needed to see Goldie and Miles and check up on my folks.

I made my way up to my parents' stateroom only to find it empty. On the door was a yellow piece of stationery that read, IF YOU ARE PAULINE SOKOL, WE HAVE GONE TO THE BOTTLENOSE LOUNGE TO HAVE A GOOD TIME. IF YOU ARE NOT PAULINE SOKOL, WE STILL HAVE GONE TO THE BOTTLENOSE LOUNGE. IF YOU ARE PAULINE SOKOL, YOU BETTER COME, AND MAKE SURE YOU ARE WITH PEOPLE TO BE SAFE. TONIGHT IS A SADIE HAWKINS DANCE, WHICH MEANS WOMEN CAN ASK A MAN TO DANCE. YOU SHOULD JOIN US. YOU WORK TOO HARD. EVEN YOU COULD ASK SOMEONE TO DANCE. DO NOT MISS THIS OPPORTUNITY.

I turned the note over and even though the printing got smaller and smaller (obviously so my mother could fit more in it to nag me), I was able to read, DADDY BOWLED A 200 TODAY, AND WE WENT SWIMMING ON THE DECK WHERE THOSE DARLING DOLPHINS LIVE. STOP WORKING SO HARD, PAULINE, AND COME MEET SOME NICE, YOUNG . . .

She'd run out of room before she could fix me up with some swinging single. My urge to go party had fizzled with the paper—and yes, with the knowledge that my parents would be in the same lounge. But I did want to see Goldie and

Miles, since I knew my parents were okay and obviously still having a good time.

I hoped my friends were still in their room, but figured I was wasting a trip as I knocked. Nothing. Damn. I'll bet they were at the lounge too. Neither were big gamblers, so I figured the casino was off-limits for them, and I wasn't sure if any shows were scheduled right now. Maybe Uncle Walt could be found in the casino, unless he had more ladies to dance with now that Jagger was gone.

If I saw the Lee women anywhere near my uncle, I'd lodge a complaint with the captain—after my drink would accidentally spill on one of their heads.

Oops.

An evil chuckle snuck out as I pushed the elevator button. When I got in, there were three young women dressed to the nines, and I figured they were on their way to the lounge too. One kept talking about the "hunk" male host who was no longer on the ship. They giggled, and a skinny blonde even suggested that maybe he was thrown off for doing something devious.

They all had evil grins on their faces. I couldn't listen or look at them any longer, knowing they were way off base about my Jagger. So I turned toward the glass section and watched the floors zoom by. In the solarium below, decorated in the ever-present dolphins—gold ones and purple ones—I saw a man hurrying by.

He was dressed in jeans and a salmon-colored tee shirt with a baseball cap hiding his face. But from here and what I'd seen in the pictures, he looked like Remy!

"Shoot!" I shouted and banged on the glass wall.

"What the hell is wrong with you, lady?" the redhead in the group asked.

I swung back to see them all staring and all showing far too much cleavage. "Wouldn't you like to know?" I stood tall and glared at them until they all turned away like frightened kids.

Good. At least I had some power over giggly twentysomethings. Suddenly though, that thought made me feel old, single and childless.

"How about that good-looking dark-haired man over there, Pauline? You are not getting any younger you know. You just had another birthday in March," my mother said, openly pointing to a man standing near the bar.

I groaned. "I know when my birthday is, Mother. We just celebrated it last month. And that gentleman over there would come up to my chest. Besides, he has no hair. How could I run my fingers through . . . ?"

"Pauline Sokol! You don't have to get obscene."

I laughed to myself. Sometimes it was fun to goad my mother along. At least I hadn't lost my sense of humor yet. It was difficult to get over that I'd just seen Remy—a killer and body snatcher. Reluctantly, I'd called the security folks but sure as hell did not want the FBI to come. Harwinton did anyway—when there was no longer any sign of Remy or any man in a salmon tee shirt.

I'll never forget the look the blond gave me.

Well! I'd have to solve my case soon to show him I was not some bumbling fool. I decided the guy probably was a male chauvinist who didn't think women should be investigators or FBI agents for that matter.

Not wanting to dwell on the case and murder, I looked around the room. The girls from the elevator were dancing with each other while couples lined the walls and bar. Edie had her hands full, pouring and serving until she looked exhausted.

Several ladies walked up to men at the bar and asked them to dance. Only one looked as if he refused. When he turned around, I nearly fell off my chair.

Harwinton.

I shook my head and thought, *How rude*. The poor girl must have built up a lot of courage to go ask him. He was a nice-looking guy, but had zero personality as far as I was concerned. Besides, he made me feel guilty about nothing.

I took a sip of my Coors and watched him sip what I guessed was a Scotch. My mother nudged my arm. "What, Mom?"

"Go ask him."

I looked around. "Ask who what?"

"That nice-looking man at the bar. He keeps looking at you. Go ask him to dance. It won't kill you."

I shuttered at the words. "No, I'd rather die than ask—"

Mother's eyes widened and she grabbed my arm. "What are you talking about? Michael," she said to my father, who was dozing off from too much excitement. "Michael, she said she would rather die. Why would she say that?" She turned to me before my father could process her words. "Why would you say that, Pauline Sokol? Why on earth—"

I raised my hands and jumped up. The way I saw it, I was far better off asking the Fed to dance than to listen to my mother and consequently have her pull the truth out of me as to why I'd rather die than dance with Harwinton.

Because I *knew* what being interrogated by my mother was like—

I approached the bar. Then I debated about running out the door and going back to my cabin, but when I looked over my shoulder, Stella Sokol had her radar set on me.

Damn.

I nodded to Edie and sat on the dolphin stool next to Harwinton. I really didn't want to dance and hoped my mother wouldn't come over and push the issue. "Hi, Edie. Busy night, huh?"

Harwinton stared straight ahead. I realized I didn't know his first name, just as I didn't know Jagger's. Or maybe it was his last name that I didn't know. Anyway, that coincidence was the only thing that was remotely like my relationship with Jagger.

Edie handed me a bottle of Coors without a glass. "Chicks are not good tippers," she said and then cursed.

I smiled and gave her a generous tip.

Harwinton looked at me. "So, tough investigators take their beer straight, eh, Sherlock Holmes?"

I couldn't believe my ears. I shifted and half my butt got involved with gravity, so I started to fall.

He grabbed my arm, saving me from the complete embarrassment that I would have faced.

Sherlock!

How could he have known? Naw. He didn't know. It was just a shot in the dark. A lucky guess. An insult to me. A . . . reminder of Jagger.

Harwinton was more like Jagger than I'd thought, only his hair color came from the lightest end of the spectrum while Jagger's came from the darkest—and their faces were admittedly different, although both . . . not bad.

I heard a fake cough from behind me and

straightened enough to see my mother in the mirror. She was getting up!

I looked at the Fed. "Thanks for the help. Yes, I like my beer in the bottle, not from a can, and get up and dance with me. Now!"

She was approaching like a tugboat at full speed.

Mr. Macho Fed didn't have time to think, to argue or to decline. Forget the fact that I was tugging on him. He got up, placed his hand on the small of my back and followed me to the dance floor.

As we passed my mother on the way, I heard, "Please, God, let this one work out for a change, and don't have him like *boys*."

Fifteen

I looked to see my parents getting up and walking toward the door, so I pulled away from my "dance" partner. "Thanks."

"Hold on. You got me out here. Now you have to finish."

Speechless, I stood there getting bumped by the passengers while I thought of an excuse. Nothing. Nada. I couldn't get away. So, I moved closer, Harwinton took me into his arms and led me around the floor.

We should be talking, I thought, feeling so awkward that I now wished I were being interrogated by Stella Sokol instead of where I was. Speaking of interrogation, I really could turn this opportunity in my favor, so I said, "I don't suppose you'd like to share any info with me that you think might be pertinent to my case?"

He started to speak, but I waved my hand in the

air and interrupted with, "I mean only what is related to the medical-insurance fraud. I'm not interested in the murder. Well—" My face started to heat up and I knew my pale complexion probably looked as if I'd spent the day in the sun. I looked at the water tank and saw Gilbert swim by.

I think he shook his head at me.

"What I meant to say was, of course I am interested in the murder. I mean Jackie was my roommate, even if for a very short time. She was human and no one should have his or her life taken away like that. Or in any way for that matter."

"The music stopped," he said.

I looked around the room. Oops. We were the only ones left out there. Not only had the music stopped, the band was on a break. "Why didn't you stop me?" Now I was pissed.

He looked down at me. "I tried. Several times. You kept going on and on. And I think you know that I can't share anything with you."

Put in my place by a Fed. Yikes!

I yanked free of his hold. "Okay, Harwinton. Don't think I'll be sharing anything *I* find with you."

He didn't have to say anything. The look said it all: *You couldn't legally get away with withholding information from the FBI.* Damn.

"Thanks for the dance," I said and turned to go toward the bar. I really needed a nice cold Coors about now.

"Tim."

I swung around. "What? Tim? Is he some suspect or have anything to do with my case?"

He moved closer, nodded to Edie to get us each the usual drink and said, "Tim Harwinton."

If I thought my face was red before, now it was crimson.

Damn, I thought as I made my way through the crowd, mostly to get away from Tim. He looked like a plain old Harwinton. Black suit. Short, neat hair. And when outside, I knew he always wore sunglasses. There was something about the guy that did, in fact, remind me of my Jagger.

My Jagger?

How on earth had I started thinking of him like that? I know he didn't think of me as *his* Sherlock. Before I knew it, I found myself facing the table of giggly females who sounded as if they were still talking about Jagger. I shook my head and started to turn.

A set of hands covered my eyes!

My first reflex was to elbow whomever, but before I could, I heard a voice.

"Guess who?"

"Gold, I about clobbered you one."

He let out a little squeak. "Oh, my. Oh, my. Why would you?"

I motioned for him to follow me. On the way out of the lounge I noticed Tim watching me.

Great. The guy really did have a knack for making me feel like a bug under a microscope.

Outside the lounge, I took Goldie's arm and walked him toward the elevator. "Where's Miles?"

"Migraine."

"Oh dear. I hope he's all right." I stabbed at the elevator button.

"He'll sleep it off. That Doc Peter gave him something for it."

I looked at my friend and realized he wasn't in drag. Made me smile to myself. I'd always looked past Goldie's appearance, often flamboyant as it were, and often after envying his wonderful taste. Now I hadn't even noticed he was doing "male" today.

Gold had on beige leather slacks, a light celery silken top and light brown leather loafers. He looked adorable, and I wondered how many women had hit on him at the Sadie Hawkins dance. I know I would have if he wasn't my roommate back home. The only one he told me about was Topaz. Actually they would make a wonderful couple.

"How was the charge for the medical service, Gold?" Before he could answer, the elevator arrived and we stepped inside with no particular direction in mind. "Where to?"

He shrugged. "How about up?"

We both turned toward the glass and watched

the passengers get smaller and smaller below us. I scanned the crowds for another glimpse of Remy, but no such luck.

The door opened on the top deck. I looked at Goldie, "Sure. Why not?"

"Okay. We can stroll in the . . . oh . . . my . . . God."

Goldie shrieked and grabbed me by the arm. The elevator door closed with a thud.

The empty deck lay surrounded by a fog. A circular fog like a donut. As the ship moved forward, rather slowly now, I realized, the donut moved along with it.

We looked at each other. "The Bermuda Triangle," we both whispered.

Then we walked toward the bow, looking around as much as we could. I grabbed onto the railing, "Maybe it's just a low-pressure system. Don't they cause all the bad weather?" I looked up toward the gigantic things on top of the ship—not moving. I didn't know squat about radar, but I could have sworn I'd seen them moving before.

"We're winging it, Gold."

He glared at me and swallowed so loudly I could hear. I patted him on the arm. "I'm sure the captain has everything in order. This probably happens all the time. Fog. Smog. As my mother would say." I forced a laugh and said a silent prayer that my folks hadn't noticed the odd scene outside.

"Your lying is getting better, Suga."

I smiled. "Want to go inside?"

He looked around. "No. If we are going under, I want to be the first to know."

I slapped his arm this time. "Stop that! We are not going under in this day and age." I turned my head and mouthed another prayer to Saint Theresa. "Come on. Let's sit."

We walked to the deck chairs and got comfortable. Goldie had pulled them closer to each other so we could hold hands as we spoke. I'm not sure who it made feel better, him or me. Other than us, the place was empty. Eeks. "So, about the cost of the medical care, Gold."

"I was meaning to tell you. Outrageous. If Miles didn't feel like crap, he would have argued with that Amazon of a woman that kept putting the moves on me at the lounge."

"Topaz. Her name is Topaz." I laughed. "Did anyone at the infirmary seem suspicious to you, Gold?"

He looked out into the fog and touched his finger to his lips. Goldie had on coral-colored nail polish. On him it looked good, whether in drag or not. "Let me think about that one. I was so worried about Miles that I . . . I wasn't myself."

I could imagine. I ran my hand along his arm. "Don't stress about it."

"I'm all right now. Let's see. The Amazon lady

seemed very confident. No suspicious behavior from her. Actually she was rather rude."

"You're on target with that one. How about the nurse? Who was on duty?"

"Some hunk of a guy."

I watched Goldie perk up a bit and chuckled. "Rico. Italian. Straight."

"Bi," Goldie said and this time patted my arm.

I sprung forward. "Are you kidding me?"

"Suga," he said, patting harder. "Goldie knows these things."

"Ha! I'll be damned." At least he'd lightened the mood. I flopped back down. Miles was safely asleep and mending so this outside air must have been good for Goldie—despite the fog donut. I was certain if we were in any danger, there would have been some kind of announcement.

Still, I could only pretend I wasn't uneasy. I touched my nausea bracelet as if it were some kind of lifesaver. When I looked out though, I realized the sea was calm. Unusually calm.

"Attention all passengers," came over the loudspeaker at that moment.

We sat upright.

"Due to inclement weather, all passengers are to remain indoors. I repeat. *Indoors*. No one is allowed on the outside decks."

"We better head in—"

A figure moved across the deck near the railing.

"Gold," I whispered and pointed. "Look."

The guy sent something sailing into the water. From where we were, it looked like . . . a picture frame.

When the searchlights flipped on, I noticed the salmon tee shirt. "Shit! It's him. Remy!" I said in as hushed a voice as I could.

We both jumped up and started toward him. Two crewmembers came off the elevator and began to say that we had to go inside.

Goldie yelled, "In a minute!" as we hustled down the deck, with them in tow.

"Stop!" I shouted. Remy knocked several deck chairs over as he ran. Like two high jumpers, Goldie and I made it over the chairs with Olympian skills.

I heard a noise and shout, and then turned to see the two crewmembers behind us were flattened by the trick. The others leaped over as we had.

Other than their cursing, an eerie silence filled the air.

Even the hum of the engines couldn't be heard.

When I got close to Remy, he pushed out his arm and knocked me toward the railing. Before I could see his face or say a word, I found myself leaning *over* the safety barrier, with my feet inches off the deck—and holding on for my life!

I screamed.

Then Goldie screamed.

Then one of the crewmembers grabbed onto my legs while Goldie yanked me back.

I melted into a puddle of fear while the fog clouded around us.

When I was able to comprehend that I'd nearly gone overboard at the hands of a killer, I looked up.

Tim Harwinton stood above me with a crewmember. Damn. He'd saved my life. Now I'd owe him something.

I pulled myself up to stand. He'd stuck out his hand, but I brushed it away. "You following me, Harwinton?"

Goldie was shaking so hard that I had to hold him in my arms.

I think Harwinton grinned, but the fog made it difficult to see. The donut had shrunk somewhat, and now encompassed the outer section of the deck.

"I have to continue my rounds. Please, all leave the deck," the crewmember said, and turned and walked in the other direction.

Tim nodded at him and then looked at me.

I didn't think there were any other passengers crazy enough to be out here besides us. I looked at Tim. "Did you see him?"

"The crewmember?"

"Remy," I said through clenched teeth. "Remy Girard."

Tim looked at me. "You saw Remy *again*?"

I ignored the tone and said, "Yeah. So did my friend, Goldie. How the hell else do you think I ended up halfway over the railing? Going for a midnight swim?" I introduced him to Goldie, making sure to point out that he was a *senior* investigator and repeating that he'd seen Remy too. When Goldie stuck out his hand to shake Tim's, the coral nail polish sparkled in the spotlights.

Damn.

Talk about a lack of credibility. I could see it in the Fed's face. But he was polite enough, and when Goldie gave his version of the story, it matched mine. Obviously the fog had hidden Remy enough that we truly couldn't identify him positively. We told Tim where Remy had headed though.

"I'll check it out," Tim said and started to move past us. "Get inside, Sherlock Holmes, before you almost fall overboard again." He said to me.

My eyes widened. I had to bite my lip so as not to shout a curse into his foggy direction. How could he call me that?

The spotlight blinked out. Goldie and I hugged each other and walked toward the elevator in the dimness.

"It's a good thing I was following you," came from the grayish mist of Tim's direction.

Back in Goldie's cabin, we made sure Miles was still sleeping comfortably, while Goldie poured himself a stiff Scotch and handed me a bottle of Coors. "You are too interested in him. That Fed guy. There's a sexual tension that is thicker than that damn fog."

I wanted to shout, but looked to see Miles snoring softly. "You're nuts. Tim Harwinton is a bore. A Fed and a jerk. Besides, he thinks I'm nuts and shouldn't be working a case since I'm female. Macho male chauvinist."

Goldie swigged his drink. "I didn't get that. Didn't get that he was chauvinistic, Suga. I can always tell. Serious about his job. Yes. Chauvinistic. No."

I sucked in a breath and blew it out very slowly.

Goldie was a genius with reading people. I knew he was probably right, but wasn't about to admit that. I liked thinking ill of Tim.

He deserved it.

"Stop letting cocaine Jagger mess up your head, Suga."

I flopped back onto the couch. "Oh, no. Not that 'Jagger is like cocaine lecture,' Gold. I can't take that right now."

He jumped up and wrapped me in his arms. It wasn't the same as a motherly hug—more a combination of parents. How I loved good old Gold.

"I won't say another word. I won't remind you of my warning that he'll make you feel good and then hurt you." He took out a pretend key from his pocket, locked his lips and threw the key toward the door.

"You've been hanging around Uncle Walt too much," I said, since my uncle always did that when my sisters and I were kids, and even now as we were adults.

Goldie chuckled.

Miles stirred.

I shut my eyes and told myself my dear friend was way off base this time.

I was not interested in Tim. No way. No how.

Goldie was just plain wrong, wrong, *wrong*.

Sixteen

Once back in my room, I undressed, stuck on my pj's and tucked my exhausted body into bed all the while telling myself how wrong my dear Goldie really had been.

Tim! Ha!

The problem was, each time I shut my eyes, damn Tim Harwinton appeared like a video on the insides of my eyelids. Probably the FBI had some kind of mind-altering system that allowed them to do that. Yeah. That was it. An FBI trick.

"Shit," I mumbled as Betty walked in the door.

"Sorry, luv. Did I wake you?" she asked.

I sat up and pulled the covers tighter as if they were some kind of security blanket. "No. I wasn't asleep yet. Betty, have you seen outside? The fog?"

She waved her hand. "Don't worry." With that she headed into the loo and left me hanging.

Don't worry, *because* the ship is going to sink,

and we are all going to die very soon anyway? Or, don't worry, because the fog is nothing, and certainly the captain can handle it and the instruments are all working peachy. Or, don't worry, because . . . I had nothing for that one.

I had duty tomorrow, so I really needed to get some sleep. I needed to forget about the night, the fog, seeing Remy, the fact that Tim thought I was nuts and that I nearly fell overboard.

This time when I shut my eyes, Jagger appeared.

And I had one of the best night's sleep onboard.

Since I was so thankful to wake up and see the ship had not sunk overnight, I sat up to look out the window. Clear in a million as they say. Perfect.

I jumped out of bed as quietly as I could, so as not to wake Betty. Hurriedly I got ready for my duty and went to eat in the crew's dining quarters.

I sat with Topaz. "Morning. How are you?"

She took a sip of her black coffee. "Ah. Much better now. I may make it after my caffeine fix." She laughed.

I smiled. "Tea drinker." I held up my mug. Then I wondered if she would ask why I didn't tell Doc Peter not to get me coffee the other day. Thank goodness Topaz seemed too wrapped up in her cup of coffee to notice. "I understand one of my friends had to go to the infirmary last night. Migraine?"

Topaz set her mug down. "Oh, yeah. The gay couple. Sweeties. I loved the way the . . . well, the one in sparkly clothing was so worried about his friend."

"They are wonderful. Both of them." I forced a laugh to keep the conversation headed in the direction I chose and didn't want to get in to her putting the moves on the "male" Goldie. "I'm glad they didn't give you a hard time. Miles is a nurse, and sometimes medical people like to tell others how to treat them."

She lifted a slice of toast and bit off a very tiny piece for such a tall woman. For some reason I would have expected a healthier bite. "Perfect gentlemen. Both of them."

I laughed. "Even when you gave them the bill?"

Topaz dropped her toast. It splashed into her coffee. "Damn it! Now I'll have to wait for another cup to cool to the perfect temperature." She got up and wiped coffee off her black top.

"I'm so sorry!" I tried to help wipe but she pushed my hand away.

"It wasn't your fault, Sokol." With that she turned.

Damn it, she was getting away. "Topaz, sorry about upsetting you with the bill question."

She stopped and turned. "Who said that was what upset me?"

I looked at her. "Oh. Sorry. No one."

The Amazon had just lied to my face.

* * *

After two bloody noses from a collision in the
swimming pool, I had to spend more time con-
vincing the twentysomething females that neither
would need a nose job, nor would their collision
have any other effect on their beauty.

I rolled my eyes after that one.

The rest of the morning was quiet enough except for a chest pain that turned out to be indiges-
tion. I made sure I was nearby when Topaz
handed the bills to the patients.

Both girls flipped out and said their parents
would be looking into this. The chest pain wasn't
upset. Odd. Then I looked at his bill when Topaz
went to put the guy's Visa card through.

It was considerably less.

Hmm. Did she have a tiered system in place depending on the patient's complaint? Although it
was good that she didn't upset the guy with chest
pains even if they were from too many spicy Buf-
falo chicken wings last night (according to his
wife), it did seem odd.

And whose idea was it anyway?

Who actually made up the rules for the scam?
Was Topaz part of it, or just an obedient employee
who did what she was told?

Damn. So many questions.

I looked to see Topaz busy on the computer and
wondered if she was working on fraudulent bills.
Doc Peter had nothing to do after finishing his

notes about the chest pain, so he headed out to the pool with his family. Since he was always on call, he could do what he wanted most days and didn't have to sit in the infirmary as the nurses did. I got up and went to the kitchenette.

When I looked at my cabinet, a chill raced up my spine. Remy really was somewhere on this ship, despite what Tim said. I think he was just miffed that the mighty Feds had not found the killer yet. I poured what little coffee was in the pot down the sink and stuck on the fixings for a new, fresh pot. Topaz must have a perfect-coffee fetish, so I decided I'd use that in my favor.

After the gurgling and spitting of the steamy liquid, the scent filling the entire room, I poured out the first mug for her. If I brought it to her now, apparently it'd be too hot. So I set it on the counter and decided to wait a few minutes.

No sense in wasting time, I thought, so I poked around in everyone's cabinet but found nothing more interesting than Betty's English scones. Blueberry. Yum. If I was a dishonest person, I would have pilfered one. But instead I walked to the back of the room, where the door led to the elevator.

Thank goodness we didn't have to airlift the chest pain out today. I said a quick prayer of thanks that chicken wings and spice were the cause and not something more serious. When I turned to go get the coffee, I heard a noise. A *thud*.

Sounded like someone being pushed. Then there was talking. Also sounded like it had come from the elevator.

No one used that elevator unless it was an emergency.

I leaned forward and tried to listen through the crack in the door.

"You can't . . . get . . . with that." The voice was probably male, but I hadn't heard every word.

The answer was clearly unintelligible, but I think female. Too quiet and muffled to tell.

I stuck my finger out to press the elevator button.

"I wouldn't do that if I were you," came from behind me.

I swung around.

"Oh, Peter. You startled me."

"What are you doing? Lost?" His hair was wet, probably from the pool.

I looked around. "Damn. I think you are right. Isn't this the elevator to the lower level?" Duh.

He looked at me. "Lower level of what?"

I wanted to say the ship, dummy, but bit my tongue. I knew what he meant, and he must have assumed that I was confused. "I was trying to get to the little café that has goodies. Like croissants and cookies. I thought I'd treat Topaz." Her coffee was probably cold by now.

Peter eyed me for a good few moments then straightened me out on my directions. I thanked him and stood for a few seconds, trying to hear more talking. Nothing. Peter started to turn.

"Whereabouts does this elevator go?"

"Only up to the top deck. It's the emergency elevator." He pointed to the sign above.

EMERGENCY USE ONLY.

If the lettering were any bigger, folks could read it from land. Speaking of land, I changed the subject. "How's the weather out there now?"

He wrinkled his forehead. "Excuse me?"

"The pool? Is the sun out now? I understand it was foggy before."

"It's fine." He turned toward the kitchenette with me close behind.

I picked up Topaz's coffee.

Peter opened his cabinet and took out several snacks of chips and cookies. Most likely for his kids. He poked around in the cabinet and cursed.

I didn't think Peter ever cursed. He looked too geeky to even know half the words that I knew.

"Something wrong?"

"I'm sick and tired of this. Someone keeps eating my Melba toast."

I wonder why sat on the tip of my tongue, but I said, "Really? Maybe they don't know it belongs to you."

He glared at me. "We all have our private cabinets, Pauline. No one steals from a coworker." With that he was gone with his loot.

I leaned against the wall to let him by and then remained there in thought.

No one steals from coworkers—unless he is hungry and can't come out in the open to find food.

I set the coffee down in front of Topaz. "I thought you might like a pick-me-up."

At first she looked confused as if no one ever did nice stuff like that for her. Then she smiled. "Thanks."

"No patients right now?"

"Uh-uh." She took a sip of the coffee and said, "Perfect. Thanks."

"No problem. Hey, how about a nice sweet treat with that? I'll run down to get it."

"I have stuff in my cabinet."

Maybe not, I thought, and waved my hand. "No problem. My treat. Nothing like a fresh-baked cookie. How's that sound?"

"Umm." She sipped her coffee.

When the door opened to the elevator, Hunter got out. I made it seem as if I was in a hurry to get in, but he managed to ask me to meet him in the lounge tonight. If I yelled that I wouldn't be caught dead with him since he fired my Jagger, it might ruin my case. So I stepped inside, agreed and when he was out of sight, pressed the UP button and made a face at him through the closed door.

I needed to see who was on the upper deck where the helicopters landed.

Just whose voices had I heard?

After only two wrong turns, I walked up a set of stairs to find the highest point on this end of the ship. There before me sat a pool (which I was told had to be drained for emergencies), a few lounge chairs, and the elevator door with another gigantic "Emergency Use Only" sign.

No one was in the pool. Since it was exclusively for the crew, only those on a day off would use it. Not very large, the water was clear blue and deep enough to dive into. I hurried around the side to see if anyone was at the far end. The rays of the sun glistened on the water and soft music played from the speakers attached to poles near the pool.

Near a bar was a small group of people—all in white—staff.

Maybe whoever was talking in the elevator had mingled into the group. I walked closer and hoped that Topaz would not page me with a nasty "My coffee is almost done. Where the hell is my cookie?"

Rico swung around. "Hey, Pauline. How's duty?" He sat with a nice-looking guy, mid-thirties, and maybe gay. Maybe bi. I still couldn't believe that about Rico, but didn't doubt Goldie's instincts.

"It's fine. Not busy at all. I'm on my break," I said, as if to justify why the hell I'd be on this deck, in the sun and heat. At least that eerie fog wasn't engulfing me now. I glanced at the radar and other equipment on the top of the ship.

All were moving now. At least the ones that were supposed to move.

Phew. One less thing to worry about.

Claude Bernard was sitting on a lounge chair near Kristina and Betty. All laughing and drinking. I couldn't tell who was with whom but guessed they were all off duty. Even Edie and the safety officer, William Benoit, were there.

I sensed I just wasted time and a trip up there.

When I smiled and turned to go, I noticed a brown woven beach bag near Rico—with a salmon-colored shirt spilling out.

Seventeen

For a second, I wished Jagger were here to shove my chin back into place. I know my jaw had dropped open when I noticed the salmon shirt in Rico's bag.

"You all right, Pauline?" he asked.

I could tell he'd followed my staring to his bag. "Oh, fine. I just—" My finger, as if having a damn mind of its own, pointed to the bag before I could pull the uncontrolable digit back. "Fine. Nothing wrong."

He pulled out the shirt. "Oh this? You staring at this?"

I shook my head.

The guy next to him laughed. "What a night that was. We all partied so hard in Bermuda—" He unrolled his towel and pulled out the exact shirt.

My eyes widened.

"—we all bought the same damn shirt. As if we don't have enough time wearing a freaking uniform." They both laughed.

I smiled, very weakly, gave an even weaker chuckle and turned around.

Several of the crew had the same salmon-colored Bermuda tee shirt as Remy Girard.

Great. Just great. Can't wait to share that with my buddy, FBI Tim.

Maybe I never really saw Remy.

Maybe he jumped ship in Miami.

Maybe he was onboard and kept wearing his shirt, just like the others—to get around the ship.

Maybe to commit another murder.

Mine.

Gulp. Walking as if my feet were magnets and the floor made of metal, I made it to the elevator and punched the button. When the door opened, crewmember Adam Watt, obviously off duty, came walking out, wearing his salmon Bermuda tee.

My break was over, so I had to head back to the infirmary. Luckily, Topaz hadn't beeped me, so I know there were no passengers to treat at the moment. Even so, I ran back as fast as I could and stormed in through the glass doors.

Her head flew up. "Geez. It's only you."

"Sorry. I got hung up. Any problems while I was gone?"

She shook her head and looked at my empty hands. "My coffee is all gone."

"And no freshly baked cookie. I am so sorry. I'll make it up to you. I promise." Damn. Hope she wasn't miffed at me.

She smiled. "I'll forgive you this time, since you make a perfect cup of Joe."

We laughed, and I felt as if a balloon of stress had popped inside me. "Can I help you with something?"

She hesitated. "Well, since there are no patients now and you don't have any crew physicals scheduled for this trip, sure. Come here." She motioned to the other violet chair on her side of the reception desk.

After several minutes, I got the hang of what Topaz had instructed me to do. I was stuffing envelopes with insurance information.

There is a God and he kept his eye on me.

And good thing I made perfect Joe.

I touched my beeper camera, which I now kept in my pocket, and kept working until Topaz got up. As she headed to the powder room, I thanked the gods that coffee had diuretic effects and pulled out my beeper.

The top seven bills on my pile were for outrageous amounts. I figured most passengers didn't complain because they had no other choice of medical treatment when out at sea. They couldn't "shop around" for better service, as Topaz had said—that was for sure.

Then, someone working here must be sending the claims to the insurance companies, getting the money back to the New York office and keeping part of it. There had to be a contact in that head-quarters' office. I kept looking through records and files and before long . . . bingo.

I had the proof.

After taking pictures of the fraudulent paper-work, I heard the clatter of spike heels on the linoleum floor. Topaz was returning.

"Any problems?" She gave me what I thought was a suspicious look.

I held up my pile of envelopes. "Nope. All done here."

"Great. It's almost time for shift change any-way. I appreciate your help—without it I'd be staying late to finish these."

Hmm. "Really? I would think they could wait until tomorrow."

She rolled her eyes. "Nope. House rules. They have to be ready to be dropped in the mail at the next port of call."

Why? "Gee. Who makes the house rules?" I asked, then chuckled to lighten the mood.

Topaz was about to speak, but from behind me a voice said, "The captain."

I swung around to see Doc Peter. "Oh. Of course he does. He must make all the rules around here."

Suddenly I wondered if Captain Duarte was in on the take. Was he the mastermind of the fraud, in addition to running this gigantic ship?

The doc went into the backroom and I watched Topaz gathering up her purse. "Hey, Topaz, I just wondered about that guy with the chest pain. Did he ever come back?"

"Nope." She bent down, picked up her shoes and slipped them on. I hadn't even noticed that she took them off when she sat at the desk. No wonder. Her feet had to be killing her.

"One thing I did notice"—We'd be docking in Bermuda soon, so I decided to give it a shot—"is that the chest pain's bill was considerably less than those girls who collided. And less than the bills I just stuffed."

She glared at me.

Oops. "I couldn't help noticing." I laughed. She didn't. Yikes.

She shrugged—and it looked genuine. "Different treatments I guess. As I'd said, I don't make the rules around here, Pauline, I only follow them. Like any good, dedicated employee should do." With that Topaz turned to head toward the door with a "have a nice night" and let Kris in as she went out.

I sat for several minutes pondering all I'd learned—and her tone.

* * *

Once I'd reported off to Kris, I went back to my cabin to change for the night. I still had to meet Hunter. Damn it. When I walked in, I froze.

Betty lay sprawled on her bed, obviously napping, but also wearing her damn salmon tee shirt! Instinctively, I checked to see that her chest was moving up and down—thank goodness.

Visions of a dead Jackie popped into my head.

Quietly I went to my closet and looked at my clothing. I didn't want to appear sexy for Hunter. Yet, I didn't want to look frumpy either, which might seem too obvious that I was angry with him for getting rid of Jagger. So, I went with ivory. Nothing sexy or frumpy about ivory.

The top I grabbed had three-quarter-length sleeves that were made of some transparent material. Hence not frumpy. The slacks that Goldie had picked out were actually Capri-style with a little lacy trim at the bottom. At the bodice of the top was a gathered section, which hugged my chest in all the right places. Hence the sexy part.

Betty snored softly as I went into the bathroom to change. I kinda wished she would wake up so we could chat a bit before I left, so I took my time, putting on my makeup as instructed by dear Goldie. What a wiz the guy was with makeup!

Finally, putting on the last of my mauve lipstick, I looked in the mirror—and thought of Jagger. Damn. *I wish he could see me*, was my first thought. Then I chastised myself and refused to admit that the guy was just as addictive as Goldie had said.

"Shoot. I'm going to have fun tonight, no matter." With that I opened the door with such force that it flew out of my hand with a *bang*.

"Bother!" Betty flew up in her bed.

I hurried over. "I'm sorry. The door flew out of my hand."

She curled her lips at me, and why not? I had awakened the woman from a deep sleep. "Really, Betty. I am so sorry."

Yet, that may have been to my benefit.

She flopped back onto her pillow and hugged her other one. She sighed and said, "Look, girlfriend, don't be barmy."

I gasped. Had Betty been that angry with me? And what the heck did "barmy" mean? I had no clue but it didn't sound good.

She chuckled. "Silly. Don't be silly. I know it was an accident. The blasted door gets away from me just about every time I come out of the loo."

"Oh." I laughed.

She looked at me. "Don't you just look smashing. Some chap is going to be pretty pleased tonight. Are you going to the lounge to dahns?"

Dahns? What the heck? I thought for a second then realized what she'd said. "Dance? Yeah. I guess I will. Hunter is meeting me there."

I looked at my watch. Five minutes late already. Damn. But work came first. "Hey, Betty. What's with all the different bills in the infirmary?"

"I'm sure I don't know what you are talking about, Pauline."

Let's hope not. "Sorry. I helped Topaz with her work. Geez. Some people get outrageous bills and others, depending on their conditions it seems, get decent, normal-for-the-treatment bills."

Betty's eyes widened. "What?"

I explained a bit more.

She sat up and listened with the interest of a grandchild listening intently to a story told by his nana. After several minutes, I said, "So you never noticed the differences?"

"Blimey. I never did anything with the bills. Topaz or the other clerks do that work." She bit her nail a few times. "I have no idea why the difference."

I shrugged. Suddenly I realized that if I made a big deal about this, Betty might get suspicious of me. Why the heck should I care about the billing? "The only reason I mentioned it was because the two girls who collided were furious. I just want to know how to handle things if it happens again."

"I'm sure, mate." She got up and walked to the loo. Before she shut the door, she said, "Ask the captain about it if you really are that interested. And have a smashing time with Hunter!"

I forced a smile. Ask the captain? Even though he knew who I was, if he had anything to do with the fraud—and I kind of doubted it—what the heck would he tell me and what the heck would *happen* to me then?

I poked at the elevator button and stepped in when the door opened. Two of the crew that I'd met in the hallway get-together the other day were there. One whistled.

I laughed. "Hey."

They both nodded and smiled.

When the door closed, the elevator started up instead of down. I must have been too preoccupied with my life's possibly being in danger to notice I'd gotten on the wrong one. We also must have hit the "milk run," because the damn thing stopped at every floor on the way up.

The two guys got off at the top and five swinging singles got on. Three females. Two males. I thanked Saint T that I wasn't one of them. That my life was so full with my career I didn't have to go out looking for a guy.

I was fine by myself. Happy. Very happy.

Despite what Mother thought.

Smiling, I turned around so as not to eavesdrop on their chatting and watched the people in the lobby below. Three guys walked across the lobby in the damn salmon tee shirts. Funny that

I'd never noticed them before. Then again, it might have been that I was only looking at single males running or looking suspicious. I had to teach myself to be aware of *everything* that went on around me.

I thought I was doing pretty well on the case by myself. A feeling of pride settled inside me. I had to brush up on being more aware and keeping up the good work.

The elevator stopped and one of the females cooed, "The Bottlenose. Last one out buys drinks!"

That cleared the elevator at record speed. I stepped out before the door shut and noticed Hunter standing by the doorway talking to one of the crewmembers.

"Hey," I said as I approached. "So sorry to be late."

He turned and smiled then introduced me to Jack, who was one of the waiters in the lounge. Apparently someone had complained about his not serving them fast enough. Some females. My money was on the darn Lee women.

I nearly suggested Jack "spill" their next round of drinks on them, but instead, I swallowed back my revenge and followed Hunter into the lounge.

The place was packed tonight, with not a foot of dance space left and all the tables taken. Around the back of the room and surrounding the tank were people standing in lines, drinking, chatting, laughing.

The lounge was swinging.

I gave a wave to Gilbert as he swam buy, then pulled my hand back feeling foolish. I swear he smiled at me though.

Hunter put his hand on my lower back and led me toward the bar. Two seats were empty but had drinks in front of them. My Coors Light in the bottle and Hunter's Scotch on the rocks. My feminist side should be miffed that he assumed that he knew what I wanted, yet I needed a swig of the cold beer right about now—and it was kind of nice to have it there waiting.

"Pauline, help yourself to your drink. I have to go appease some of the passengers. I'll be right back though." He bent forward.

I eased back a bit, but he managed to kiss my cheek. I wanted to smack him and yell that he shouldn't have gotten rid of my Jagger. Instead I mumbled that was fine and thought to myself that he could stay away all night and I wouldn't care.

Edie came over and chatted a few minutes, but she was so busy she couldn't stay long.

"This seat taken?" I heard from behind.

"I'm afraid it—" I swung around to address the guy then stopped. "Do you Feds have jurisdiction over dolphin bar stools? If so, have at it."

Tim chuckled and moved Hunter's glass to the side and then sat. "I'll leave when he comes back."

I was about to say don't, but then Tim would

think that I *wanted* him to stay! Ah, the dilemmas of dating. The swinging singles could have them.

"Hey, I found something out today." I told him about the damn tee-shirt follies and took a swig of my beer.

He seemed to ponder what I'd just said.

"You don't think I've seen Remy at all, do you?" I said.

He looked at me over his glass while he drank. "Do *you*?"

Damn it. I blew out a breath. "I was so sure that I had, Tim. I mean after finding his stuff in that room and seeing him in the picture, I was sure. Besides, who tried to throw me overboard?"

"It was a foggy night, Pauline. The deck was very slippery. Maybe you slid toward the railing when you ran after what you thought was Remy. Or it could have been that you surprised whoever it was and couldn't clearly see him because of the weather."

That was a possibility. I polished off my Coors and waved to Edie. "You want another one?" I asked Tim.

He looked taken aback that a woman would even ask that, and I remembered that he probably didn't think I should be working a case either, despite what Goldie had said about him not being a chauvinist.

So, I proceeded to tell him all that I found out about the billing. Tim seemed very interested and even made a few notes. Suddenly I felt more like we were working together, and it felt kind of nice.

I looked in the mirror behind the bar, and all of a sudden, I felt a chill race up my spine.

Stella Sokol fast approached.

"There you are, Pauline. My goodness, it has been so long since Daddy and I have seen you. We've been to the movies, two shows, Daddy won a hundred dollars on the slot machines and I won three."

"Dollars?"

"No, silly. Three *hundred* dollars." She patted me on the arm. I wanted to ask who she was and where was the real Stella Sokol. So far, she hadn't even acknowledged Tim or tried to fix me up with him.

Then the world screeched to a halt.

Mother leaned over and gave Tim a hug!

I started to introduce them, but the words stuck in my throat.

Mother waved at me as if erasing what little I could say midair. "Don't be silly, Pauline. We've met. Dear Tim—" She looked at him and I think gave him a kind of sexy smile.

I looked away too fast to see the entire incident, twisting the muscles of my neck in the process. "Ouch!"

Mother ignored me. "—would I say 'interrogated' Daddy and me, Agent Harwinton?"

I gasped.

Tim chuckled. "*Questioned*, Stella. *Questioned* is fine."

I pushed my hand past my mother's arm and grabbed Tim on the sleeve of his—what else— dark gray suit. "You *questioned* my parents?"

"Take it easy. We questioned everyone onboard, Pauline. You should know that."

I let go and sat back. It dawned on me that my parents knew about Jackie's murder and hadn't summoned me to their cabin to stay with them the rest of the trip. Edie hadn't brought my drink yet, which turned out to be a good thing. Probably I would have downed it in one gulp.

"Daddy is still in the casino, having the time of his life. I'm just here to find Goldie and Miles. They are meeting us for dinner on the upper deck. My treat." She laughed.

I was about to check her forehead.

Stella Sokol had to be feverish.

"I haven't seen them," was all I could manage. Living in the Twilight Zone had taken away all my intelligence. Sitting silently for a few minutes, I watched Tim and Mother converse, then she kissed him on the cheek, gave me a wave, said she was glad I was with him for safety and was gone.

Who was that woman?

I needed pine-scented Renuzit.

And I needed my mother back to normal!

Maybe the fog of the Bermuda Triangle had

had some kind of paranormal effect on her. I only hoped Daddy and Uncle Walt were not affected too!

After what seemed like hours but had to be only a few seconds, I looked at Tim.

He smiled and gave me a look like, Why can't you be as carefree as your mom?

"That is not really her!" I yelled above the tango music. "That's not my mother. Stella Sokol does not . . ." What was I doing?

"She's not really your mother?" I could see a faint grin as he took a sip of his drink.

"Of course she is. I'm sure you know all about me, down to my parking tickets."

"Tickets? Unpaid? How many?"

"Never mind. Are you going to question them anymore?" I wanted *desperately* to change the subject.

If only I could have Gilbert the dolphin swim me back to Connecticut.

Hunter came up from behind and cleared his throat.

"Oh, hi," I said. "Everything all right with the Lee women?"

His eyebrows rose. "How did you know they were the passengers that complained?"

Because you threw Jagger off the boat because of them. "Let's just say . . . I've met them and it was a lucky guess."

He looked at Tim and said, "Fine. They are happy and everything is fine. Now we can enjoy our *date*."

Tim stood and picked up his drink. "Actually, I have to borrow Ms. Sokol for a few minutes. She's the last on my list to question."

My eyes widened. I wanted to scream that I had nothing to do with the murder and that I'd already given statement after statement. But if I did that, I'd have to stay with wishy-washy Hunter, who placated passengers like the Lee women.

So, I smiled and said, "I'm really beat too. As soon as Tim is done with me . . . is done asking me questions, I'm going to head back to my cabin. Thanks for a nice night." Nice night? I hadn't spoken two words to Hunter, but it seemed an appropriate goodbye.

Once out of the lounge, I grabbed Tim's arm. "Look, I've go nothing more to tell you about Jackie's death. That night I told you guys all I knew. All I'd seen. I have no motive other than once I caught her painting her toenails on my bed."

With a typical FBI solemn face, he took his notebook out of his breast pocket, pulled out a little pencil like the one I'd gotten from Uncle Walt's golf bag and sneaked into a mental hospital on my last case, and started to write.

I froze on the spot.

"Color?" he asked.

"What?"

"What color nail polish?"

The old phobia of being arrested when I was not guilty sped through my Coors-affected mind. "What . . . what are you . . . I didn't do . . . Tim, you have to believe . . . I had nothing—"

All I could hear was the pencil clatter to the floor while Tim's lips covered mine.

If this was part of being arrested, maybe I'd never seek treatment for that phobia. Being arrested wasn't as bad as I thought.

It was actually quite delicious.

Eighteen

With Tim's lips still on mine, my mind went blank—except for the shear pleasure of the tingling feeling sailing throughout my body.

Slowly he pulled back and looked at me. Not as a Fed though. Nope. More like a man. A man who seemed . . . interested.

I thought he might apologize for the kiss, but instead he just smiled, and I think mumbled the word "nice." I couldn't help but sigh, and then said, "I hope that's not the way you question all your possible witnesses."

He chuckled. "No. It isn't."

I was glad he didn't use some clichéd line like, *Only the pretty young ones.* "Good. Because I was starting to have visions of you and Stella . . . never mind."

He laughed and took my arm. "You really that tired, or would you like to get a coffee?"

If I admitted I wasn't tired, he'd know I was blowing off Hunter. Then again, who cared? "Coffee sounds like too much caffeine, but decaf tea would hit the spot."

He shook his head slightly and smiled. Then he led me toward the elevator and pressed the DOWN button.

Jagger popped into my thoughts, doing his head-shaking thing, but it wasn't the same—at least that's what I told myself. How could I compare the good-looking but clean-cut, shorthaired Tim with the dark, dangerous, delicious Jagger?

I couldn't or shouldn't, so I decided I wouldn't.

On the elevator, Tim kept holding onto my arm and it felt nice. If I were in the habit of doing one-night stands, like some of my friends, this would be an opportune moment.

But I was Pauline Sokol, good Catholic girl whose conscience would have her mumbling inco-herently if she did something so out of character.

Still, the kiss was wonderful.

Tim leaned over and kissed me on the cheek this time. When we were nearly at the bottom floor, I looked out the window and dreamily said, "Ha. There goes another Remy look-alike in one of those dumb salmon tee shirts."

I guess an FBI agent is never really off duty. He

pulled back, looked out the window, and said,
"Shit!"

When the door opened, Tim was out before me
in the proverbial flash and running across the
lobby. I stood in shock for a few seconds and then
headed after him.

It really *was* Remy!

Had to be.

I took in a deep breath and was glad I'd been a
jogger for the last thirteen years. Before I knew it,
I was running through the doors after Tim, and
the clatter of footsteps on the metal stairs
sounded ahead. A door opened and shut below.

Tim cursed and jumped over the railing, just
making it to the staircase below before he fell to
the bottom deck. Yikes! He was through the door
before I made it down. When I opened it, I saw
him at the end of the hallway, which led out to
one of the lower decks.

"Tim!" I shouted, but when he turned to answer, I watched a lounge chair come flying
through the air—and smack into the back of his
head. I screamed and ran faster as I watched him
fall to the ground.

He was out cold. I grabbed my linen handker-
chief from my purse and put pressure on the
wound. It wasn't too big, only a small gash, but
damn head injuries bled a lot worse then they
were. Hopefully he didn't have any brain trauma.
"Tim. Tim!"

He opened his eyes. "What the hell?"

"Good. You're alive."

"Is that what you'd call this?"

I took his hand and placed it on the handker-chief. "Hold this really tightly. I'll call for help." I hurried to a phone on the wall, called the infir-mary and told Rico where we were. "You all right?" I asked, hurrying back.

"I'll live," Tim mumbled.

"Good. Stay here."

I ran ahead and around the curve of the deck—then froze when I heard a splash. I looked over the railing; Remy was in one of the lifeboats, pulling the starter on the motor and then sailing off.

Foolishly, I shouted to stop.

He looked at me and gave me a third-finger salute.

When I got back to Tim, I knelt down beside him and pressed my hand on his. "I got it now."

He looked at me. "Where'd he go?"

As Rico and two other crewmembers came rushing over to us, I shut my eyes for a second and whispered, "You don't want to know."

After Tim was stitched up and told me for the hun-dredth time that it wasn't my fault that I had called his name, making him turn around, I walked him to his cabin, where he promised to stay put until morning. I still think he blamed me though, but he didn't act like it. He was that good of a liar.

The other agent was called and instructed to keep waking Tim through the night to make sure he didn't have a concussion and remained coherent.

On the way to his cabin, I told him about the lifeboat, and we realized that Remy, being a long-time crewmember, knew how to get it down and use it.

I also thought that now I was much safer on-board, but didn't voice that tidbit to Tim.

Probably he still thought that I never saw Remy.

Inside Tim's cabin, which, by the way, was huge, with a balcony and two rooms (courtesy of the taxpayers?), I helped him to the couch near the windows. "Can I get you something?"

He shook his head and then said, "Damn it!"

"I don't recommend shaking. Doc Pete will have a look at those stitches tomorrow and make sure your brain wasn't involved."

He looked at me.

I raised my hands in the air. "No comment. I'm certainly not going to tease you after you've been injured with some low-blow brain joke." I sat next to him and asked, "You think Remy is headed for Bermuda?"

"We're set to dock there by morning. So, I'm sure he is. My partner sent word ahead to the authorities to be on the lookout for him." He leaned back and sighed. "We'll get him."

I was dying—no pun intended—to find out if Tim was convinced that Remy was the killer. But he looked rather worn and even a bit pale. I took his pulse, out of habit, despite his protests and led him to his bed. He slipped out of his suit jacket, shirt and slacks while I turned around, and I tucked him in.

When I noticed his reflection in the mirror opposite the bed, I couldn't help but bite my lip to keep from swooning. The guy was built like a brick wall and had tattoos on both upper arms. From here I couldn't see what they said, but one was clearly a sun design. Neat. They really looked neat and sexy. Who would have thought Pauline Sokol would go for a guy with tattoos?

Come to think of it, Jagger had to have one or two somewhere on his body—I'd just bet he did.

And promised myself that some day, I'd have my answer.

Once back in my cabin, I sat on the edge of my bed and thought about tonight. Betty had the night shift, so the place was all mine—and that meant no snoring with a British accent. I did feel horrible about Tim getting injured though. Not to mention the fact that Remy got away.

The only positive thing was, he was running like a guilty man, which made all our work and Tim's head injury all worth it.

I got up, headed to the bathroom to change and was soon snuggled in my bed. When morning came, we'd be docking in Bermuda—and I'd never been out of the United States.

I couldn't wait!

Warmth touched my face, causing my eyelids to flutter. I rolled over, grabbed my pillow and said, "I'm not going to school today, Mom."

Had I said that out loud? Ha! After a few seconds, I started to chuckle. Then I felt around my empty bed with my hand and suddenly missed my darling Spanky. He was always good for a hug or a laugh—what a canine sense of humor he had—and I could talk to him about anything.

Not that he gave a damn about what I said, but that unconditional-love thing always kicked in.

With thoughts of Spanky stuck back in my mind, I realized there was no movement. Not that I'd felt the ship much—thank goodness. But we must have stopped.

I flung myself up on my knees and looked out the porthole.

Land!

Across the street, and I do mean the ship had pulled into the dock like a car parking along the sidewalk, was row upon row of shops. Colorful, typical Bermuda—from the tourist brochures I'd read—shops. Bright pinks, beiges, yellows and even blue buildings. The Harborfront Restaurant.

A perfume shop. A jewelry store. Several clothing boutiques and even an Irish linen shop. How neat!

I couldn't contain my excitement as I jumped up and pushed the porthole open more. With just about sticking my head out, I could see gigantic ropes holding the ship in place. Reminded me of a doggie chain holding the monster of the sea from escaping. And the small cars were driving on the wrong side of the road! Well, I told myself, for Bermudans it was the correct side, but it sure looked odd to a New Englander.

With a laugh, I got up, danced around my cabin and then pulled clothing out of my drawers and closet. Thank goodness Kris had let me have the first day in port off and took my shift.

After all, the rest of the medical crew had been here a gazillion times. Feeling very much the newbie, I donned my white shorts—Bermuda length—and a dark pink sleeveless top, and grabbed my Steelers visor and sunglasses. First I lathered my face, arms, legs and neck with heavy-duty sunblock. As much as I'd love a nice tan, I wasn't a fool. My European ancestors had blessed me with skin as fair as ivory and hair as light as sunshine—without added chemicals.

Soon I was on my way to breakfast with the crew. I hoped I'd see my parents sometime today. I figured I'd more than likely run into them and Goldie and Miles, since Bermuda was not a gigantic island—and besides, passengers had to stay on the part of the island where the ships docked.

Rico was eating near the doorway with a few of the other guys. All wore the stupid salmon shirts.

"Hey, *amore*, how's it hanging?" he asked, then laughed.

I rolled my eyes and chuckled. "Let me get my food and I'll join you."

He pushed an empty chair forward. "No problem, but I think your buddy would rather you joined him." He pointed a finger toward the other side of the room.

Tim Harwinton sat there sipping coffee and reading something.

I wanted to shout that he wasn't my buddy, but I actually felt some kind of attachment to him. You know, in a *friendship* kind of way. After all, we were both investigators of sorts. "Let me go see if he's all right."

"Doc Pete checked him out this morning. One hundred percent cured. No problems."

"Great news, Rico."

He nodded and took a bite of his toast. One of the crewmembers at the table gave me a dirty look, as if I should leave Rico alone. Glad that Rico had someone interested in him, I smiled inside. Despite my earlier little talk with myself that I didn't need a man, maybe I did *want* one.

It would be nice to have someone to share a laugh with, a stroll along the beach—and maybe a few *other* things.

"Hey. How do you feel today?" I pulled the chair out and started to sit across from Tim and then stopped. "Oh. Do you mind? Am I interrupting?"

He looked up. "No, and no." He motioned for me to sit. "And my head is fine. The doc checked me out."

"So Rico said." For a few seconds, I felt foolish sitting there with not even a drink while he kept his nose in his paper. I lifted my head enough to see it was a map.

I guessed of Bermuda.

Obviously Tim was never off duty when on a case like this. "That Bermuda?"

He nodded. "Ouch."

"You can't shake your head after being injured like that. So, you are looking at a map of Bermuda to find your way around?"

Tim looked up.

Duh. I felt so stupid. "What I meant was—"

He leaned forward. "I know what you meant, Pauline." He touched my hand.

Yikes! He knew I meant to make small talk since I was a bit nervous around him? *Of course, Pauline, he's the damn FBI!* They know everything—or at least give the impression that they do.

"Don't let last night interfere," he said.

Last night? Did he mean the injury? Chasing Remy? Or . . . the kiss?

"I . . . do you want some more coffee?" I got up way too fast and knocked his cup over and what little he had left. "Sorry!" I grabbed several napkins and started to wipe the table, his hand, and the damn map, now a soggy mess. "Oh, shit. Look at your map."

He looked at it, looked at me and pointed to his head. "It's all in here. Don't worry." He got up. "I'll take a rain check on that coffee. I'm meeting someone and can't be late." He leaned over and took my hand.

Geez. I felt some kind of heat in his skin. Wow.

"You be careful. I don't want you walking around alone." He gave me the once-over.

I was glad I had chosen an outfit that didn't make me look frumpy.

"By the looks of you, you're heading off the ship. Do not go alone. Stay with some friends, Pauline. Remy is out there, and we'll be picking him up."

Did I say frumpy? I felt like Joe Tourist. When I looked at my arm, a streak of sunblock hadn't soaked in yet.

Now I was glad that Tim had to hurry off.

I gathered up my tan woven shopping bag, my sunglasses and my hat, and then started toward the elevator that went down to the main lobby where the passengers disembarked. I got into the elevator and went to push number three, but stopped.

Damn Tim's words were so loud in my head that I actually looked around the elevator to answer him back. Instead, I poked the Down button to go back to my room. I'd see if Betty wanted to walk around with me. We only had half the day here in Bermuda, and I hated to waste time.

Our room was empty when I got there, so I called Goldie and Miles's room, certain they'd taken off as soon as we'd docked. I mean duty-free shopping! No answer. I flopped on the bed and tried to talk myself out of calling my parents. For a while, nothing convinced me—other than not wanting to ruin my first trip out of the country—but then I realized I didn't want to put them in harm's way. Yes! That was thoughtful, logical and gave me the creeps thinking that Remy was out there and maybe after Pauline Sokol.

I wondered if he would recognize me and if he knew I'd been following him around with Tim. He had to have guessed Tim was FBI by now. Maybe Remy thought I was too.

Yeah, right.

I grabbed my bag, looked out the porthole and sighed. I had to get out into the swing of things fast. Staying in public places would keep me safe. After all, I had my pepper-spray necklace and a few tricks up my sleeve that involved the self-defense moves Jagger'd taught me on another case.

I was set for the day.

As I made my way up to the main lobby to get off the ship, I looked around at the opulent golds, purples and whites. The place looked like a ghost ship. I figured everyone was out shopping or sightseeing.

I headed to the corridor that led to the gangplank. Smiling at a crewmember stationed there, I asked, "Any recommendations for a good meal?"

"The Harborfront has fresh seafood, a sushi and tempura bar too. Very good." She then introduced herself as Judy Mik.

She had the same British accent as Betty. I looked out the door to see that at the end of the gangplank there was a pink-and-white balcony of sorts. I figured I'd have to pass through the Customs building to get cleared to enter Bermuda.

In the parking lot below were tiny cars (compared to the SUVs that I was used to seeing in New England) and rows of mopeds. Little motorcycles. Maybe I'd rent one and ride around the island.

"Have a wonderful day," Judy said.

I waved to her, walked down the plank and stopped to look around. The air temperature was perfect. Somewhere in the seventies with a sea breeze, I guessed. A faint salty scent filled the air, horns honked on Front Street below and people chatted while sitting on the pink walls of the balcony ahead.

I turned to see how the mighty *Golden Dolphin* looked from this angle—and gasped.

Directly above my head hung the red-and-white lifeboats, all lined up in a nautical row— with one gaping hole.

From the one Remy had stolen to come to this island.

Nineteen

I could barely contain myself when I
stepped onto the sidewalk in Bermuda.
This was so much fun! Maybe being a cruise-ship
nurse wasn't such a bad gig after all.

Wait, what was I thinking?

Any nursing job was out of the question, and
when I got back to the States—that sounded so
cool in my head—I was going to tell Fabio not to
give me any more nursing cases. I'd burned out of
that career and couldn't take the stress of the job
any longer. Apparently, thirteen years of nursing
was my lucky number. One day, when I found
myself being attacked by a flying throat swab shot
from a five-year-old's mouth, I decided I'd had it.
No more staffing problems. No more almost exclusively working with females, who could be
catty and gossip until hoarse, and no more watching patients suffer and not being able to help.

I really wanted to help people.

I was putting my foot down.

Learning more and more about how to investigate, I was sure I could do other fraud cases and not have to take these damn jobs.

Let Goldie do the medical.

When I looked at the bustling traffic, on the wrong side of the street, the men in Bermuda shorts with suit jackets and ties, and the obvious tourists with arms loaded with shopping bags, I decided to forget my problems and just shop.

No one ever had to tell me twice to enjoy myself shopping.

"Ha!" I said as I passed a litter can. Even *those* were classy on this island. They were painted in delft blue and decorated with some emblems that looked very royal. As colorful as the buildings were, I noticed that many of the vehicles, like little versions of our vans, were mostly white. How Bermudan was that?

It seemed a bit confusing, crossing the street with the cars on the opposite side from what I was used to, but I made it to the "land side," where all the shops were located in a long row along Front Street.

In the distance, I noticed a guy with short blond hair in a suit.

Tim?

I weaved in and out on the crowded sidewalk until I got close enough to see the guy's legs. No way would Tim be the type to wear Bermuda shorts with a suit. Just didn't seem like Bureau attire to have your legs showing—no matter how good they looked.

I laughed out loud and a few people turned to stare at me. Much like a kid in a candy shop, I bustled along, going in and out of different shops and wishing that I had a bigger budget to spend on myself.

My stomach was telling me it was getting close to lunchtime, if I hadn't already missed it. Tempted to go back to the ship for a free crew's meal, I started down the street toward the boat.

"Oooooooh! Marvelous!"

I stopped dead in front of Roxzy's Fashions & Novelty Boutique—and started to laugh.

"Suga! Come see this smashing outfit," Goldie called through the open door.

I shook my head. "I heard you all the way down the street, Gold."

He stood there in his Marilyn Monroe short curly wig, a sparkly black-and-white top—the black in a spider-web sort of pattern—and a long black skirt.

Looked as if he should be accepting an Oscar.

"Gold, that is you." I walked closer and looked at the price tag of a few items. A handbag was way out of my league and so was a silver necklace that I wouldn't even put on my Christmas list, since no one in my family could afford it.

"This shop is you, Goldie. It really is. Where's Miles?"

He chuckled. "We split up awhile back. We're meeting for lunch at the Harborfront Restaurant down the street. Want to join us?"

I thought about how that crewmember Judy had said it was a good place to eat, but she hadn't mentioned price. *Really*, I thought, *I should treat myself*.

Goldie leaned near and kissed me on the cheek. "You've been working way too much lately doing both jobs, Suga. Come to a nice lunch with us. My treat."

I gave him a peck on the cheek. Two of the sales clerks glared at us. It was so easy for me to look past the exterior where Goldie was concerned and to see the real person inside. It hadn't dawned on me that I looked as if I had just kissed Marilyn. "I'm there," I said and laughed.

He said he'd only be a minute, paying for his purchase. I told him I would meet him there, since I needed to get some more sunblock. The bottle I had was expired and I'd read that it might not be as effective. After another quick peck, I went out and left Goldie fawning over a hat that he'd just discovered.

Laughing, I looked in various store windows to find a place with suntan lotion. Many of the shops were boutiques and clothing seemed the most popular item around here. I passed a shop called

Wadson's and thought it looked the most likely place to find sunblock.

There was a crowd inside, which made me conclude it was also one of the less expensive places to buy souvenirs. Some tie-dyed tee shirts caught my attention. They'd look great on my nieces and nephews, but I really couldn't afford to buy something for everyone. I settled for a colorful mug for Adele. She was the best receptionist I'd ever known, and since we often had coffee together with Goldie, I thought it an appropriate gift.

I went to pay for it and ask the clerk where they might have sun block. The line nearly snaked out to the door. I only hoped Goldie and Miles wouldn't get worried about my being a bit late. How I wished our cell phones worked over here. Man, how we really relied on them.

I kept looking around the shop while the clerk worked as fast as she could. The Bermudans' British accents made me smile and think of Betty. Too bad she wasn't able to come shopping with me. Finally a young man, pierced from head to toe and sporting blue hair, hurried to the other cash register and asked us to form two lines.

I kept looking at my watch. I hated to be late. It wasn't in my nature. But I'm sure my roomies would understand, and thought maybe Goldie found more things to buy.

"Next," the female clerk said.

I hurried forward and put my purchase on the

counter. As I was about to ask for the sunblock, a man's arm reached in front of me to get something off the counter. Apparently he'd forgotten one of his bags.

"Cash or charge?" the girl asked me.

"Oh—" I looked down to see the guy's wrist. Suddenly I couldn't speak.

The exact rope bracelet as Jackie's!

Before I knew it, I was shouting for the clerk to call the police, while Remy—and now that I'd gotten a look at his face I had confirmed who he really was—hightailed it out the door.

I grabbed my shopping bag, knocked Adele's mug to the floor in my haste and amid the crashing clatter of ceramic heard the clerk yell that I'd still have to pay for it. "I'll be right back to pay!" I shouted.

"Yeah, right," the pierced guy said and two customers tried to grab me.

I shrugged them away, yelled something about a murderer and then ran through the crowd. This time Remy had on a navy tee shirt and tan shorts. He had to have some connections on this island where he stayed and where he could change his clothes.

"Stop him!" I shouted, but no one paid me much attention. I looked around for a police officer who might be directing traffic, but there weren't any in sight. "Damn it. Someone help me!"

I ran as fast as I could with my bag slung over my shoulder. I'd been tempted to throw it down to get more speed, but then thought I might need it to smack Remy.

Running down an alleyway, I could still see him in the distance. Something made me think of Jagger—and I reached down and fingered my necklace.

My shopping bag went flying, I formed fists with my hands and used them to help me sprint down the alley. It really did pay to exercise and jog.

The walls were decorated in island graffiti with palm trees chipping off the stuccoed buildings, but it all became a blur with my speed. I guessed the doors were the backs of shops, but kept concentrating on my suspect and my breathing.

"You don't understand, Fed!" he shouted.

I spun around to see if Tim was behind me and then realized that Remy thought I was an FBI agent. I smiled and sucked in a breath. What didn't I understand? "Then stop and explain!"

"Ha!" he shouted and sped up.

He had a point. If I was FBI I'm sure I wouldn't believe anything he said without some proof. Maybe he was trying to lure me into some scheme where he'd kill me.

Yikes!

I didn't see any point in telling him that I wasn't FBI.

Despite the pain in my lungs, I was keeping up

pretty well. I shouted a few more times as if he'd stop, make a confession and turn himself in to me. Right! Instead, he led me on a long chase, and before I knew it, we were back on Front Street, weaving through traffic while horns beeped at us and drivers yelled. Soon I found myself on the water side, which was filled with people.

Another cruise ship must have recently docked.

"Excuse me," I repeated over and over as I fought through the crowd while people gave me dirty looks. A few times I thought I saw someone that I recognized and was about to ask for some help, but then I'd get closer and even in a blur, I could see they were all strangers.

I weaved to the left and nearly knocked over a woman wearing a pink muumuu. The man next to her had on a palm-and-floral shirt. Tourists, no doubt. The lady turned so fast, she started to topple forward.

I slowed and grabbed her arm. "I'm so sor—" I let go real fast.

"Pauline Sokol! You should be ashamed of yourself, running on a crowded sidewalk like this. You nearly killed your parents."

I stood on tiptoes to see Remy still running away. "Sorry, Mom. I didn't nearly kill you."

She grabbed my arm this time. "We taught you better manners than that, Pauline."

"Yes . . . you did." Remy was nearly out of sight. "Let go, Mother. I'm working!" I brushed her hand away and made sure she didn't fall before I sprinted away. "Love you both!" I shouted over my shoulder.

"You too, *Pączki*," Daddy said.

I looked up ahead. Now it seemed like a wall of people were covering the sidewalk. Damn.

"Make way!" I yelled and jumped down to the curb. Before some little car ran my feet over though, I was back on the sidewalk. "Pregnant lady coming through!" I shouted, thinking that was a great line for getting ahead of this mass of tourists.

The crowd parted like in some biblical movie and there sat Remy—atop a bright red moped. He gave me a wink, another salute and most likely in the fastest gear, sped past me. I reached out with my necklace and gave him a spray.

"Aye!" he shouted, spun the bike and fumbled to gain control.

"Stop him, someone!" I reached out to grab Remy's arm, but he managed to overpower me.

I landed on my back, with the crowd gathering around, a few police shouting and Remy zooming off.

And my mother standing above me.

"Don't give me that look, Harwinton. It really was Remy," I said as Doc Pete put a few stitches in the back of my head.

I hoped I had a concussion, because each time I

closed my eyes, all I could see was my mother staring down at me and wagging her finger.

Tim touched my arm and winced a few times as the doc sewed me up. "I know. We were on him."

Oops.

Surely he wasn't going to tell me that I blew a federal case, a *murder* case? Yikes.

"Oh, my head hurts so badly," I lied, hoping Tim would find it in his FBI heart to ignore the fact that I might have ruined his case. "Ouch. Ouch. Ouch."

He leaned near. "I've got seven stitches on you. So I think I win the prize for pain."

What an agent this guy was. Even knew fake pain, or at least when a girl was trying to change the subject. Still, my head did hurt a bit. The cut was numb from the Novocain, so it wasn't from that. I sat up with the aid of Tim, and Peter pronounced me fine.

"But you really should rest the remainder of the day, Pauline. Make sure someone wakes you up . . . well, you know the drill," Doc said.

I nodded. "Ouch."

Tim smiled. "A wise woman once told me not to shake my head after just getting a head injury."

"Ha. Ha." I have to go back and find my shopping bag. I threw it somewhere along the chase.

Tim leaned near, "Tell me, Pauline, what exactly were you going to do with Remy if you caught him?"

"I don't like the way you said 'if.' Makes it sound as if you think it was impossible that I *could* catch him. You know, he thought I was a Fed."

He chuckled. "Come on. I'll walk you to your cabin."

"My bag—"

He rolled his eyes. "I'll go find it. Tell me what it looked like and where you saw it last."

I explained on the way to the elevator and persisted with the fact that I was in top physical condition.

Tim grinned and leaned forward. His lips touched mine ever so gently as the bell rang and the door opened.

"Saved by the bell," I teased.

He took me by the arm and led me inside. "You know, you really could have been hurt out there."

"High school basketball. The nun coach used to drum into our brains how we should keep our heads up when we fell. Worked. I only bumped my head on the sidewalk once and not too hard."

"I'm glad." This time his lips remained longer. Felt better. Hotter. Or maybe it was me. Feverish already?

"Hey," I eased back a bit. "How did you turn up on the street after I was pushed anyway?"

"Good tailing."

Ding.

The damn door opened. Tim moved aside so I could pass. Then he put his hand on my lower back, and I felt safe. Despite the fact that Remy could be running loose in Bermuda, I felt safe with my Fed near me.

My Fed?

Was I nuts? The guy merely kissed me, and here I was referring to him as *mine*. Maybe my head was injured more than I thought.

And had he been tailing Remy—or *me*?

Tim and I reached my cabin in a few minutes. I knew Betty was on duty so I dug around in my pocket for my key. "Oh, shoot. My key was in my shopping bag."

"Maybe your roommate is in?" He leaned forward and touched the doorknob.

"No, she isn't."

The handle turned in his hand. The door opened enough so I could see the chair by my bed . . . *occupied*.

Twenty

Oh . . . my . . . God!

"Er . . . no. Nope. My roomie. She's . . .
um . . . at—" I looked in my room again.

Maybe I was hallucinating.

Maybe my brain was permanently damaged.

Or, maybe what I saw in my room was *real*.

"Oh. Well, I guess . . . let's see." I looked in the
crack of the door again to be make sure.

My "guest" waved at me.

I was pretty sure hallucinations didn't wave.

I swallowed and turned to Tim.

"You all right? Maybe I should make sure you
get some rest and come wake you—"

"Nope!"

He glared at me.

I forced a smile, stood on my tiptoes and kissed
his lips. "Thanks so much. I'll be . . . I'll be . . .
er . . . fine! That's it. I'll be fine. Please go look for

my . . . Wait! No. No. Don't worry about that silly bag. I don't need it." I gave him a gentle push toward the elevator. "Shopping bags are a dime a dozen. I'll get another room key from the purser too. Don't you worry about that stupid bag."

He leaned over and kissed me back. "I'm getting worried about you."

"Ha! It would take more than a little fall to break my noggin. I'm as hard-headed as any Polack comes." I forced a laugh, sounding more as if I were being strangled. "Okay. I'll see you later. No!"

"Pauline, really. Let me—"

"Oh no, you don't, buddy. My hard-earned tax dollars are paying your salary, and I want my money's worth." I chuckled. "Go find that killer so the world will be a safer place. I'll see you later." I turned and swung back, watching the hallway spin around me. Yikes. "By 'I'll see you later' I mean call me. Call me *first*. Okay?"

The elevator door opened. Tim stepped in. As the doors started to move, he said, "Whatever you say—if I can figure out what the hell that is."

"Ha! Funny! You're a real card. Funny FBI agent. Isn't that an oxymoron?"

The elevator door closed. For a second I leaned against the wall and let out a breath. Then I pushed my door all the way open and stood there for several seconds. "What on earth are *you* doing here?"

Jagger merely smiled. Oh so very Jagger-like.

* * *

I finished filling Jagger in on the details of my case, leaving out that Remy pushed me down, but leaving in how I managed to pepper-spray his butt—well, half of it anyway.

"Atta girl, Sherlock."

As proud as the proverbial peacock, I sat on the edge of the bed and felt as if I would collapse at any moment. But I told myself that I couldn't. This case was moving fairly quickly, and as soon as Tim brought Remy in, I'd be able to question him as to who else worked with him on the fraud.

Jagger made me rest for a while since he claimed I looked pale. I had to do some maneuvering so he never got a look at the back of my head. Thank goodness Doc didn't have to cut any of my hair to sew me back up.

Even though I felt a bit "punk" as my grandma— *Babci,* we called her—would say, I wasn't able to sleep a wink. Jagger did, however, remain by my bedside, so I felt pretty darn relaxed.

"Oh, shoot," I mumbled as someone knocked on the door—and I heard my name screeched out.

"I forgot I was supposed to meet Goldie and Miles for lunch."

"Suga? You in there?"

"Pauline! We are frantic. Are you all right?" Miles asked. "We hear talking. Are you . . . oh, God. Someone is not in there harming you!"

Bam! Bam! Bam!

I looked at Jagger. "Open the door before they hurt themselves."

When he opened it, Goldie and Miles rushed in, grabbed both my hands then turned and shouted, "Jagger! Thank goodness it's you. We were worried about our girl."

Miles leaned forward. "You're pale. What happened?" He touched my hair to push it back and must have felt the bandage beneath my locks. "Oh! Oh! What *really* happened?"

I rolled my eyes and figured it was a losing battle. With Miles being a nurse, Jagger a top-notch PI and, well, Goldie being darling Goldie, I never could make up a lie good enough to fool all of them.

So I spilled my guts, including how I ran into my parents and finished with, "Hey, I never had lunch. I'm starving. Oh, and Miles, please call and let them know I'm fine."

He nodded.

Jagger stood up. "I'll go get us something to eat." He looked at Miles and Goldie. "You two stay here with her."

Great. Now he'd frightened them with his guilt order and they'd never leave.

They nodded in unison and plopped down like obedient children, one in each white chair.

As soon as the door closed behind Jagger, I said, "You guys go. I'll be fine."

Miles merely looked at me.

Goldie mumbled. "Jagger said—"

I waved my hand. No use in getting them into trouble with Jagger—but I had to get out of there soon and find out if Remy had been caught. Something told me Tim would not give me a buzz and nonchalantly say they had the guy. I know his loyalty to his job had to come first.

So, how to get out of here before Jagger arrived?

Goldie sat very still, barely taking his eyes off of me. How sweet. Every once in a while I'd smile at him.

Miles, being an OR nurse and less worried, yet definitely concerned, dozed in Betty's chair. Hmm.

I motioned with my index finger for Goldie to come near.

He looked at Miles and tiptoed over. "What is it, Suga? Need something?" he whispered.

"Actually, I do. Jagger is taking way too long. I'm dying for a Coke. I think the caffeine would be good for me right now." Good thing Goldie wasn't up on medical stuff. "I'm feeling a bit nauseous."

"Oooooooh."

"Shh!" I looked at Miles. "Please just go to the machines near the infirmary, out to the right, and get me a can of Coke. Would you be a dear and do that?" How I hated lying to my precious friend.

Goldie put his finger to his lips, motioned toward Miles and winked at me. "Done."

When I heard the door click and noticed Miles hadn't stirred, I made my move. In slow motion, which I was hoping would cause less ruffling of sheets or any other kind of noise, I got up, grabbed my shoes, and was out the door, guiding it very slowly so it wouldn't shut with a bang.

I said a short prayer that Jagger would not take my escape out on my friends as I hurried down the hallway to the left. At the end, I leaned against the wall to put on my shoes. With one foot in the air, I bent to slip one on. The elevator door opened.

Out walked Jagger!

I flung myself around a corner as fast as I could before he saw me. Remaining like a statue, I waited. Nothing. No footsteps on the carpeted floor but also no Jagger peeking at me from around the corner. Phew. I made it.

Soon I was in the elevator, all alone, thank you very much, and on my way down to who knew where.

I had to find out more about my case, since I knew Remy was no longer on the ship. And I knew Jagger, Miles and Goldie would be out looking for me any second. Where would they go first?

The main lobby, thinking I was leaving the ship.

I looked across the room to the north elevator and . . . bingo! The three of them were on the elevator going down!

Quickly I swung to the side and leaned against

the wall so they wouldn't see me. Knowing Jagger, I had to be really careful, so I slunk down below the glass, nearly sitting on the floor. I couldn't even peek out to see if they saw me. Too dangerous. So I remained there until the elevator stopped and the door opened.

"What the hell are you doing, Pauline?" Betty asked before I could jump up.

Thank goodness it was my roomie. "Oh, I fell today and felt a bit woozy." I got up. "I'm fine now."

"I heard about your fall." She still gave me an odd look. "You all right?"

"Peachy," I said and laughed. "Who told you about my . . . accident?"

"I stopped by the infirmary to get my jumper." She held out her white sweater. "Rico and Peter told me. I'll check on you throughout the night if you'd like."

"I wouldn't *like* to get woken up, but a few times may be necessary. Thanks."

She nodded. "Where you off to?"

Yikes. I had no idea. Maybe I could feign confusion. Then again, they'd take my job away from me. "Actually, with my accident, I missed lunch. I guess I'll go for an early meal."

"I'll join you. Just in case you get a bit loony." She chuckled.

I smiled and was actually glad for the company. When we got our trays of food, Betty and I sat near the window. The place was practically empty, since it was around three and so early for dinner, but the food was warm and good. We talked about our pasts and Betty wanted to know all about what it was like to grow up in America and about my nursing jobs.

I had to pretend I still worked at St. Greg's, the last hospital that I did management in OB/GYN. She seemed to buy it and told me about the jobs that she'd had. I really got the sense that Betty came from money.

"I love the way the British have their royal family, Betty. It's so interesting and historical at the same time."

She looked across the room. "My grandfather was an earl."

Wouldn't that mean his children would be royals also? I thought, but Betty didn't look open to questions. How interesting. Europeans had such wonderful histories behind their lineage.

"Wow. An earl. That is neat." We finished our meal and each had two cups of tea. Mine was decaf. Betty crinkled her nose at that and teased me that I didn't drink *real* tea. I'd never spent this much time with my roommate, since our shifts often kept us apart. After she asked me a bit more about my current job, we cleaned up our trays and headed out of the place.

"Pauline, I've always wondered how they found you so fast to replace . . . Remy. How was that?" she asked as we walked toward the elevator.

Oops. First I shivered at the thought of Remy, and then I fumbled for a lie and wondered why Betty would care. How'd she come up with the question? "That's an interesting question. I believe that my boss had connections with someone that had something to do with the ship. The *Golden Dolphin* line, that is." Oh, damn. Even I wouldn't believe that.

"Well, I'm off." She got into the elevator and really didn't look as if she expected me to join her.

I stood and watched the door close, then got another chill up my spine.

But this time it didn't have to do with Remy.

I needed to find Jagger, so I made myself obvious by going out on the deck where the passengers were embarking from their tour of Bermuda. Saddened to see the island for the last time, I had to concentrate on work, and wondered if Tim would be sailing back or staying on the island to find Remy.

"You should be ashamed of yourself."

I swung around at the sound of Jagger's voice and smiled to myself. Did I know the guy or what? "What are you talking about?"

"Involving those two in your trick. They're just about in pieces over your escape."

Damn it.

"You didn't holler at them or make them feel worse did you?"

He shook his head.

I'd have to call Goldie and Miles's room and apologize. But first I had to talk to Jagger. "Come with me."

He didn't hesitate or ask any questions, which made me feel as if he again trusted my instincts and thought I was capable of investigating on my own. We walked up the stairs to the upper deck, where the top of the dolphin tank sat.

Jake, Johnny and Gilbert were gracefully swimming in circles. I think they all stopped and smiled at me—or my head was injured worse than I thought. I told Jagger to sit on the edge of the tank and I stood near him, looking around.

Several passengers were on the far side enjoying fancy drinks with tiny umbrellas in them and some were in the pool, splashing about. No one was close enough to hear us, so I kept looking at the dolphins and told Jagger about Betty, the monarchy, whatever I could think about Remy and my thoughts.

He told me how he'd gotten a flight to Bermuda and "poked" around there before the ship docked, but didn't find anything of interest.

I wondered if he really flew there to "protect" me. Neat.

"I think there is some tie that we are missing. Some connection between whomever killed Jackie and whomever is involved with the medical-insurance fraud."

"I agree."

My mouth dropped down to my chin.

And Jagger smiled.

It felt wonderful. While basking in my glory, I waved to Gilbert, who waved his flipper at me! "How cute!" I started to laugh and tell Jagger about my aquatic friends.

Suddenly my laughter stopped.

In the darkened corner of the deck where the bar ended stood a shadowed figure—within earshot.

The sun blinded my vision so I couldn't see clearly enough to identify who was watching and listening to Jagger and me. If it was Remy, I was glad to have Jagger nearby and wondered if he was "packing."

"Well, maybe we should take a walk?" I said and motioned for him to follow.

Jagger got up and leaned near me. Before I could move, his arms were around me and his lips on mine!

Wow!

For a second, it didn't matter who was lurking in the shadows, I had *other* things on my mind. But that crazy thought only lasted a second.

Besides, Jagger whispered in my ear, "Don't look toward the shadow. Someone is—"

I should have been disappointed, but, well, this was Jagger. Workaholic extraordinaire. He must have seen the figure in the reflection of the window directly across from him. I had been busy looking at the dolphins, but that seemed to work out as a good cover.

Before he could finish his sentence, something flew forward and nearly missed our heads and the tank.

A fire extinguisher landed *smack* at our feet.

And the shadow disappeared.

"Stay here!" Jagger shouted and ran toward the other side of the deck.

I really couldn't just stand there, so I hurried to the stairwell where Jagger had gone, clasping my necklace with one hand and grabbing the doorknob with the other.

When I stepped through the doorway, I paused. Silence. No one was running on the stairs. I cautiously made my way down and tried to see if the door to the lower deck was still closing. No such luck. Maybe Jagger was doing better than I. I wondered if Remy did come back onboard to finish some job he had started.

Who else was on his list of victims?

After several hours of searching, I went back to my cabin to see if Jagger had returned there. Betty hadn't gotten back yet, but there was a note on my pillow—in Jagger's handwriting.

Oh, yeah. I noticed the small things when it came to Jagger.

For a few seconds, I thought of Tim. Tim. Jagger. Tim. Jagger.

What a conundrum.

Jagger had said he would be searching in the background, as he'd put it, and that I should stay in the open. Go to the Bottlenose Lounge and stay there, since it was always crowded.

I looked down at my outfit and decided I had to change. My first thought was to put on something comfortable with good shoes for running if need be.

Then I realized Jagger was onboard and grabbed my slinky black dress and heels, telling myself if I had to save my life, I'd fling off the shoes and run like hell in my bare feet. I did, however, leave off nylons since they would be too slippery for running. Before I was done, I hooked my pink necklace back on.

Once ready, I went out the door, looked both ways—since I didn't know if I was a target or not—and hurried to the elevator.

That same gang of giggly girls was on it and I was never so glad to see the annoying bunch. I stood silently and listened to them. One said she saw a passenger that looked like the "host" that was thrown off the ship in Miami, but the others said they saw him too and he was much better-looking.

I laughed out loud.

They all glared at me, and I said, "You had to be there," while the door opened and I scooted out.

Jagger had been correct. The lounge was packed, and I figured everyone had their fill of Bermuda and since the ship was going to set sail very soon, they all decided to party and forget the island.

"Hey, Pauline."

I swung around to see Hunter. Yikes. I hoped he didn't recognize Jagger. Then I shook my head, and thank goodness my headache was gone. I was talking Jagger here. The guru of disguise wouldn't let anyone recognize him if he didn't want them to.

Hunter insisted I have a drink with him since it'd been some time since we'd seen each other. I wanted to say it was no great loss, but had to keep my mouth shut or risk blowing my cover.

Edie poured me a nice cold draft beer while Hunter had his usual Scotch. I leaned over to Edie and said, "I'm on the wagon tonight. Coke will do."

Like a perfect bartender, she didn't question me, but Hunter looked surprised.

"Migraine earlier. Too much pain med to mix with alcohol."

It looked as if he bought that, but before I knew it, he had yanked me up and we were headed to the dance floor.

Music blared way too loudly for my head injury, but I sucked it up and moved farther away from Hunter. He kept trying to pull me closer. The dance floor became so crowded, we could barely move. Starting to feel claustrophobic, I said to Hunter, "My migraine seems to be coming back. I'll have to sit this one out."

I think he groaned in annoyance, but wasn't sure over the blaring music, the yelling and laughter, and flickering strobe lights.

At this rate I might suffer a seizure.

When I got to a "clearing," I looked up—and saw Tim standing in the doorway.

Remy must be back onboard!

I had to make my way over to him without being obvious and causing a scene with Hunter. All of a sudden, someone screamed.

I turned around and looked to where a woman in a skimpy silver dress pointed.

Jagger, eyes closed, was sinking lower and lower into the dolphin tank—with a stream of scarlet floating from behind his head.

Twenty-one

The Bottlenose Lounge could have been empty for all I cared. I ran so fast to the doorway, out into the hallway and up the stairs that the people shouting obscenities at me had no effect on me.

Jagger needed me.

When I got to the top of the stairs, I heard footsteps behind, but didn't care. I yanked the door open and ran through. On the top of the tank, sitting near the edge and holding a knife . . . was Betty Halfpenny.

Oh . . . my . . . God.

No wonder she was so unusually nice!

I grabbed a life preserver from the wall, and rushed toward the water.

"Keep out, Sokol! You two have ruined everything," she warned in a deadly voice. "Unless you want to be next." She cackled. A cackle with a British accent.

Very eerie. Kinda like Mary Poppins without manners.

I stood on the edge of the tank, ready to dive in.

Betty grabbed my arm and sliced across my shoulder with the knife.

"Ouch!" I ignored the pain and smacked her across her face with the life preserver. I hoped it left a permanent imprint. "Let me go. He'll die!"

"Then he shouldn't have stuck his nose in my business." She swung the knife again.

I ducked this time and realized Betty was not a very good fighter. Too proper, I imagined.

"I found your little camera. And some emails from a Fabio. You two have been spying on me . . . on us. Damn you, Pauline. Things were going so well until you came onboard."

I shoved her with all my strength. She stumbled to the deck. I dove into the tank, forgetting my fears, forgetting the fact I couldn't swim well, but not forgetting that by now Jagger was probably lying at the bottom of the tank.

The crystal clear water didn't prove a detriment to my swimming lower. I couldn't yank the life preserver down so I hung onto the rope and let the donut part go. It floated to the surface of the tank.

My lungs hurt worse than when I had run after Remy.

There, below, was Jagger, limply floating like a piece of seaweed.

I pumped my legs as hard as I could, and before I got closer, his body was propelled toward me, then past, then upward.

In awe I watched Johnny pushing Jagger's body to the top. I turned, tightened my grip on the rope, and tried to swim upward. My lack of oxygen fought me all the way, until I felt something poke into my back. At first I feared Betty had thrown her knife down then looked to see my buddy Gilbert pushing me upward!

We reached the top of the tank in a second, a whoosh of air flew from my lungs and a deep intake of breath kept me conscious. Before I could thank them, I grabbed onto Jagger and pulled him to the edge.

The door to the stairwell swung open. Tim and the other agent rushed out—followed by Remy!

"Help!" I splashed the water to get their attention. "Tim!"

Suddenly Betty got up and flung the knife at me. It was the dolphin-handled steak knife. In her fury, she nicked my other shoulder with it. I swung around to see the knife splash into the water.

"You bitch! Now you're in trouble!" I shouted, and then gasped. "I'm not going down after that, you know."

Tim grabbed Jagger and lifted him over the side while the other agent pulled me out with the aid of several crewmembers. I heard a cough, a gurgle of water and, "Sherlock. Is she—"

Tears mixed with the tank water on my cheeks. "I'm fine. I'm fine." With that I collapsed into the surprised agent's arms.

Under the watchful eye of an armed Tim, Doc Peter stitched up both Jagger's and my wounds. Sure it felt odd to have your doctor being guarded at gunpoint, but out at sea now, we had no other choice.

Peter had killed Jackie.

Betty had freaked out and told Jagger about the killing when he confronted her by the dolphin tank and accused her of medical-insurance fraud. Being ever so proper, it made it difficult for her to accept the nasty accusations—and it wasn't true.

I'm sure Jagger skillfully goaded her into confessing more and more. I only wished I could have been there to hear—and help him, but he'd said Betty was insanely in love with Remy and really wasn't involved in the fraud.

Her obsession had been only for Remy, and she hated Jackie because Jackie had found out—and teased her about her feelings, along with saying that Remy would never love her. Betty knew it was true. She'd had a past filled with weirdo boyfriends and never had found her real love.

"Ouch!" I said as Peter yanked on my arm.

Tim and Jagger both moved in as if for the kill.

Through clenched teeth Tim said, "My finger could just slip, buddy," while Jagger said, "Don't hurt the lady, Doctor."

Oh, boy. Just what I needed. Stitches under pressure. I wondered how gigantic the scar would be.

I smiled to myself, lying on the exam table, Rico and Kris at the side and a sterile green paper sheet around my neck and back to keep the area germ free. I'm sure Peter couldn't make one tiny slipup with all the watchful eyes around me.

I peeked up at Jagger. "What about Peter's wife?"

"She and those kids were hired family. Actors, who knew nothing of the fraud or murder. Imagine. The guy had planned to have them come on-board as decoys. This way, he could make the moves on Betty behind the scenes while in the open professing to be a loving husband and father. Who would suspect a nice family physician to be involved in fraud? Peter thought he'd covered all the angles."

"Stop talking about me as if I'm not here," Peter whined.

Oh, boy. I could see that gigantic scar on my back now. "Well, Peter, you should have thought about the kind of attention you'd get when you killed Jackie," I said. "Ouch!"

Tim looked down at me. "It might not be a good idea to antagonize the suspect while he's stitching up your shoulder."

Despite the pain—I swear Peter only gave me half the numbing drug on purpose—I laughed.

"I'll put the dressing on," Rico said, pushing Peter out of the way. I think he wanted to smack the guy, like the rest of us had the urge to do.

Peter slumped into a chair next to Betty, who sat like a proper statue under the guard of the other FBI guy, whose name I never did learn. A few of the crewmembers stood at their sides. Although Betty was handcuffed, Peter took her hand into his.

She glared at him and pulled back. "Blast you, you birk!"

Yikes. I had no idea what that meant, but I was guessing Betty didn't have the same feelings for Peter as she had for Remy.

Spurned love sure can mess things up, I thought, as Rico helped me to sit up.

"Stay put a few seconds to make sure you don't get woozy, *amore*." He kissed my cheek.

Tim and Jagger took a step forward.

After a few minutes I proclaimed I was fine and got up. With only one stagger, I landed in Jagger's arms, with Tim still holding his weapon on Doc Peter. The safety officer was now handcuffing the doc.

What a sad, wasted life. He could have been a prominent doctor, but after going bankrupt by being greedy in his practice and having a penchant for overspending, he devised this insurance-fraud scheme and involved his coworkers onboard the ship—and Betty, the woman he professed to love. According to her actions, she didn't love him back, but Jagger said she sure loved the illegal money that he showered on her.

Her family had been wealthy until her father had an affair and ran away—with his inheritance. There went his title and Betty's family's income. That's why she took money from Peter—no matter where it had come from.

Peter had fallen for Betty on his first cruise as a doctor on the *Golden Dolphin*. The more he persisted, the more Betty grew to hate him—since it interfered with her trying to accomplish the impossible—to snag Remy away from Jackie. But being so crazy in love, Betty never gave up trying.

However, Jackie, the consummate risk taker, went along willingly with the fraud scheme. I'd bet for the thrill of it and not as much for the money.

Remy, in fact, turned out to be the innocent one. That's what he'd been trying to tell me in Bermuda. He'd found out about the fraud and had reported it to the captain who in turn told the insurance company fraud unit. After snitching,

Remy thought it best to go under cover himself, because he worried about Jackie's involvement, so he disappeared—hence my job. That's why the papers were in his file box.

But since he was so in love with Jackie all the way back to their days in nursing school, he must have gotten scared she'd get caught. So he tried to convince her to get off the ship with him at the next port and never look back. In fact, he may have broken some law there.

Typical for Jackie, she'd refused. However, Peter had gotten wind of Remy's interference from Betty, who had her own agenda involving Remy. Peter worried that Remy's love could influence Jackie and she'd rat him out . . . so he'd taken care of her. No way could a dead woman blow their good deal. Peter then took the opportunity to get rid of her body in the sea, as if that would prevent him from being found out and tried for murder.

Betty, whose life was built on revenge from never having the lover she'd wanted, aided Peter in anything that would hurt Jackie. However, he swore Betty didn't know about the murder plan.

That night in the fog, she had dressed in the salmon tee shirt and threw the picture of Jackie and Remy overboard—then consequently tried to add me to the fishes' diet. In the weather, we never noticed she wasn't as tall as Remy, but she was as wide.

I looked down to see she had on a similar rope bracelet to Jackie's. Peter must have taken it off the corpse and given it to his love. Eeyeuuw. Was it any wonder that Betty didn't return Peter's feelings?

While under cover on the ship, Remy, truly wanting to help his Jackie find happiness, had managed to find out that their land connection was one of Peter's old girlfriends, and that Peter had set her up with the job in the New York billing office. Once Jackie was killed and all eyes had focused on him, Remy thought he could never come clean and convince anyone that he was innocent.

It had been Jackie's handwriting on the chart, calling poor Claude a cheat because he dated one of the hairdressers onboard. He was lucky not to have gotten involved with Jackie.

Look what had happened to Remy.

I glanced at him as he stared at Peter and Betty. Sorrow filled Remy's eyes, and I wished things could have been so very different. He finally caught me staring at him.

"I'm sorry. About your head. Pushing you. I thought you were a Fed or something. That's why I ran. No one would have believed me if I told them the truth. I just needed more time to prove it." He looked from me to Peter. "He killed my Jacqueline." Tears ran down his cheeks.

I walked over and gave Remy a hug. "I know. I know."

Betty yelled at me to get away from *her* Remy.

Tim shouted for her to shut up at the same time Jagger did.

What's a girl to do with two men so very protective of her?

I laughed inside, and once the safety officers came and removed Peter and Betty from the infirmary, Rico and Kris cleaned the place up.

The captain had said that if there were any injuries that needed tending to by the physician, Doctor Peter was to be taken from lockup and, under the constant watchful guard of the FBI and security crew, treat the passengers.

I wondered if we were going to sail at warp speed to get back to New York and back to our normal lives.

Hope Valley was looking really good right about now.

There really was no place like home.

Tim came forward and looked at me. "I'd be proud to work a case with you again, Sherlock Holmes." He kissed my hand and held it in his for a few minutes.

Yikes! I thought Jagger was going to explode.

Then Tim took me into his arms and kissed me so very gently on the lips. I couldn't even look at Jagger after that. I hugged Tim and whispered, "Me too. Me too."

With that he was gone. Jagger looked at me and said, "Well . . . you . . . you did good, Pauline. You did good."

Although he usually only used my real name when he was pissed or deadly serious, this time I knew it came from the heart (not to mention the fact that he surely didn't want to use the same nickname for me as Tim had), and Jagger was nothing if not honest.

I took him by the arm and said, "Come on. Let's make the most of this cruise. I want you to meet three friends of mine."

And off we went to see Johnny, Jake and darling Gilbert.

Experience other
comical and clever adventures
of nurse turned p.i.
Pauline Sokol

**The
World of Lori Avocato**

A Dose of Murder

Pauline Sokol's adventures first began in this hilarious debut novel, so open wide and say AHHHHHHHHRRRGGGGHHHHHhhhhhh-hhhhh!

After years of chasing around sniffly munchkins with a tongue depressor, nurse Pauline Sokol has had it. She's sick of being an "angel of mercy"—she'd like to raise some hell for once! But finding a new career won't be easy for someone who's had no experience beyond thermometers and bed-pans.

Luckily, the smarmy head of a medical insurance fraud agency hires her, mostly because of her killer pair of legs. Soon, Pauline is going undercover as a nurse at a local clinic, and the healers around her start drop-ping dead! Luckily, the hunky and mysteri-ous Jagger is there to step in and teach her the ropes before her own continued wellness is in jeopardy!

The Stiff and the Dead

Pauline has a drug problem . . .

Pauline's second case finds her going undercover at a senior citizens' center, where prescriptions are being filled for a patient who just happens to be dead. A little snooping reveals that the recently deceased oldster was up to his jowls in an illegal Viagra ring!

Not that Pauline begrudges these elderly gents their newfound virility, but it becomes a bit unnerving to be in the middle of a group of sex-mad lotharios, especially when people keep turning up dead! Hopefully, her handsome co-worker Nick and the enigmatic Jagger will make sure that the next prescription for murder doesn't have Pauline's name on it!

One Dead Under the Cuckoo's Nest

Former nurse-turned-insurance fraud p.i.
Pauline Sokol's current undercover investigation into a sleazy scam has hit a small
snag: She's been forcibly committed to a
mental institution! Pauline's certainly sane,
but try telling that to the nuns who run the
place. Even her cohort Jagger is unwilling to
spring her until she digs deeper into the
scam that the mental institution is running.
When the strange death of a gender-
confused "sister" further complicates matters, Pauline realizes she may need the help
of her own very kooky family to find a way
out of Wacko Town . . . alive!